Acting

Acting

a novel

sherri winston

MARSHALL CAVENDISH
NEW YORK   LONDON   SINGAPORE

Text copyright © 2004 by Sherri Winston
Marshall Cavendish, 99 White Plains Road, Tarrytown, NY 10591
www.marshallcavendish.com

Library of Congress Cataloging-in-Publication Data

Winston, Sherri.
Acting : a novel / by Sherri Winston.— 1st ed.
p. cm.
Summary: Longing to escape from her small Michigan town, sixteen-year-old
Eve, an aspiring actress, is forced to confront both her family's and her own
expectations when her twin sister announces her pregnancy.
ISBN 0-7614-5173-0
[1. Sisters—Fiction. 2. Twins—Fiction. 3. Identity—Fiction. 4. Sex—Fiction. 5.
Mothers and daughters—Fiction. 6. Michigan—Fiction. 7. African Americans—
Fiction.] I. Title.

PZ7.W7536Act 2004
[Fic]--dc22
2003027123

The text of this book is set in Lomba
Book design by Alex Ferrari/ferraridesign.com
Printed in The United States of America
First edition
1 3 5 6 4 2

KENNEDY

Acting

Act One

Scene One

Either the town is shrinking or my breasts are getting bigger!

God, how Eve wished she were anywhere else. Anywhere other than Eden. Her hometown. Eden with its boarded-up businesses. Eden with its smallness pressing at her back, her legs, her head. Eden squishing the life out of her.

Eve sighed. Her head was hanging over the back-porch steps. She squeezed her eyes shut and pressed her fingers against her temples. When she tilted her chin toward her breasts, she said mockingly, "I'm going to hell, and it's all because of you."

Eve pulled herself to her feet and shook her fingers and hands until the blood circulated again. When she stretched, she felt her breasts press against the soft fabric of her sweater, and a memory flashed that almost made her laugh.

At nine years old, Eve had actually prayed for breasts.

Prayed, "Dear Lord, please bless me with nice ones—breasts, I mean—and I promise I'll never ask for anything else."

Well that had been a lie, of course. Indeed she'd prayed for plenty since the days when she'd thought that if she had enough cleavage, she could face any challenge, solve any problem.

Cleavage couldn't save her from Eden. And it couldn't make her mother and sister love her again.

She gazed beyond the wooden porch columns that framed the yard. A soft breeze rippled through the pale green leaves that speckled the backyard. Flat, white sky stretched without a single cloud as far as she could see. A beautiful day for the first week of November. Michigan autumns along the lakeshore were usually cold by now. Eve watched the leaves, savoring the tickle of warm air, then bit her lip as her mind skipped from her silly, long-ago prayer for breasts to what she desperately prayed for now: forgiveness.

After the mistake she'd made last spring, Eve prayed she could make things right. She prayed God would send her some sort of sign.

Back in April, Eve had messed up. Bad. Bad enough to cause harsh words and deep sobs and theatrically slammed doors. Bad enough to set her mother and father against one another. Bad enough to drive a wedge between Eve and her twin sister.

Eve crossed the porch to the ironing board. When she was stressed, she ironed the laundry that had piled up all week. In the future, Eve would thank the makers of her favorite starch when she went up on stage to accept an Oscar for her starring role in a brilliant movie. As she pressed the iron against a pillowcase, she got an odd, tingly sensation.

A chill?

The heavy front door creaked loudly. Slammed. Windowpanes jitterbugged in their frames.

Eve pictured how she looked, her face warm and soft from steam and fading sunlight. If this were a movie, she would be in the center frame with the camera panning in closer . . . closer . . . *Is my hair OK?* But then . . .

Eve spun around, saw her mother—not a tall woman but still a few inches taller than Eve's five foot nothing—coming through the kitchen door. Her mother's face was filled with pain, the way she had looked when Eve's body had started to develop ahead of her identical twin's.

"You knew about this, didn't you?" Ma barked in Eve's direction as she came out on the porch. Eve stumbled backward, toppling the neat stack of linens she'd built with her ironing, and fell to the floor.

"What, Ma, what?" Eve wailed.

"Stop your acting," Ma said. *She always says that,*

Eve thought. And Eve's silent retort was always the same: *The last thing in the world you want is for me to stop acting. Otherwise you might have to stop acting, too!*

Just then Eve's twin sister, Eve, came through the swinging doorway that separated the kitchen from the living room. Eve and Eve. Ma used to tell the girls that, just like Rebekah in the Bible, she had prayed and prayed to be a mother.

"God answered my prayers," Ma told the two girls when they were little. "Just like Rebekah, He blessed me with twins." Eve Alexandra and Eve Belinda. Eve Alexandra, at thirteen, came home one day and with typical intensity announced she would no longer answer to "Eve" because "having two Eves is stupid. Call me Al from now on," she said.

Right now, Eve's mother stood on the porch, panting and venting steam like the hot iron. She did not look like a woman blessed.

"Ma, try some anger management," Al said, coming outside. Al's eyes locked with her sister's. "Eve's the last person I would have told."

Ma brought her hands to her face and covered her eyes with her fists. "I wish to God you hadn't told me, either." She stomped inside, brushing past Al and disappearing through the swinging doors to the living room.

"What?" Eve said. "What did you do? Why is Ma so, so . . ."

"I'm going to have a baby," Al said, her voice as soft as the Indian-summer air and flat as the pale November sky.

Eve shook her head, not believing what she'd just heard, but Al said, "You heard right. Having a baby. Me."

"Are you serious?" A sharpness crept into Eve's voice that surprised even her. She scrambled to her feet. Al's face darkened.

"Don't look at me like that," Al said.

"Like what?" Eve gulped. Back in April, Al had hissed: *After everything else, now you do this? How could you? I hate that I'm your sister.*

The memory crawled along Eve's spine.

Al appeared exhausted. Hoarse, she whispered, "You're still not better than me. We'll always be different." Then she turned and walked away.

That night, falling asleep on crisp, fresh sheets wasn't easy. Eve heard her mother come into the bedroom and shut the window above her bed.

Eve's body remained in a tight coil until Ma left the room.

When Eve rolled over, frosty air from the once-open window made her shiver. A huge, saffron moon shone into the room with a sugary glow.

A baby.

Al had no boyfriend. What in the world would she do with a baby?

Eve bit her lip, praying for some sort of direction.

Passing headlights painted the walls of Eve's room. Shadows appeared to dance and move. Then the car rolled away, leaving the shadows motionless. The dancing stopped.

A hiss, then a sigh of night air sent a cloud jumping over the moon. The mild weather was leaving.

Winter felt cold and near.

Scene Two

Two days after Al's announcement, pellets of ice slanted across the sky and hit the roof of the car. Eve rode in the passenger seat beside her mother.

"Bet this'll be a rough one," Ma said, nodding toward the window. She was referring to the weather the way everyone in Eden spoke of the weather.

Obsessively.

Inside her head Eve heard herself shout, *Who gives a flying, fat damn about the stupid weather?* Deep breath. In light of Al's . . . situation, Eve was working overtime to convince her mother that she was a good girl and could be trusted. So she did not shout her true feelings about how stupid she thought it was to talk about the weather. Instead she said, "Maybe it won't be so bad this year."

Ma pulled up next to the grocery store and shoved a list into Eve's hand, her fingers lightly grasping Eve's wrist. "I'm babysitting Benny and Nick for Eugenia, so I have to pick them up. Be back in about thirty minutes." Eugenia, a fellow church member, had lupus, and Ma often babysat her boys.

Ma's breath steamed up the window, but not before her gaze followed Eve's. Lucious Prior worked at the Golden Apple Grocery. Eve heard her soul groan, *Mmm, Lucious!*

"Eve!" Ma's voice crackled.

"OK, I won't forget anything," Eve said, afraid to make eye contact.

Ma's fingers lingered on Eve's wrist as Eve took the grocery list with her other hand. Eve couldn't avoid her stare. "Please tell me you're not that stupid," she said. "No daughter of mine could be dumb enough to consider the likes of him. Right?"

Ruth Ann Noble, queen of the close-ended question. Eve had been fed her line, knew her line; nothing remained except to say her line.

"I know, Ma," she nodded.

"And you look ridiculous in that hat. Couldn't you find anything more ladylike? That thing won't even keep your ears warm."

Eve looked at herself in the side mirror as she slid across the seat and out the door. The navy hat with white horizontal stripes resembled something out of a Dr. Seuss book. A bold, dynamic statement of whimsy, she'd thought. Something her mother would instantly loathe. A good girl's rebellion must always be masked, never straightforward.

"I'll be ready when you get back, Ma," she said, casting her eyes downward but not before noticing the severely crisp points of her mother's white shirt, which Eve had starched to within an inch of the garment's life.

Eve watched Ma drive away. Head down, she walked slowly by Lucious. Beautiful, sexy, gorgeous Lucious, who invaded her night dreams and her daydreams. Thinking of Lucious was one of the few things that filled her up and took over her whole being as much as her desperation to leave the small town. Eve mumbled hello without looking. She kept moving, walking past him as fast as any good girl could.

Scene Three

Scene Three

Three weeks had passed, and Eve sat reading in the kitchen.

Daddy had come home a week earlier and was heading out with his truck again. Several nights in a row, when Eve was in the bathroom, she had listened through the heating vents as her parents, in the next room, begged and pleaded with Al to tell them the name of her baby's father.

Al always gave the same answer: "Never!"

Now Eve shifted in the kitchen chair and pushed the once-hot cup of tea away. When Eve had heard her mother use her extra-special Authority Voice to ask Al whether she'd consider having an abortion, Al had started to sob.

A tightness settled in Eve's chest, and she blinked hard, as the pages of type began to blur. Shakespeare. *Othello*. She was reading it as part of one of Mr. Harris's famed "English projects." Eve set *Othello* aside.

She found it hard to concentrate. Through the beautifully framed, perfectly paned windows that her father had so proudly hung with his own hands, the outside world was navy blue. Eve believed her entire view of the world was forever framed by the rear, kitchen window. She had spent most of her life looking out that window and wondering what life was like outside the yard, down the tiny road leading to the highway, and beyond.

Dear Lord, what am I going to do if Al goes away after she has that baby?

What would her life be like once the baby was born? What would any of their lives be like? Al had made one thing clear: she still planned to graduate ahead of schedule, still planned to attend college in the fall. Eve turned away from the window and stared down at *Othello*, a story of betrayal. Al was going to leave her behind. . . . The tightness returned to her chest. When her breasts had spurted a full two cup sizes larger than Al's, it physically marked an unmistakable difference between them.

Al countered with her big brain, skipping a grade. Now she was prepared to graduate a year before Eve.

"Belly," Daddy's voice boomed, startling her. Daddy was deaf in one ear, and his voice often rose louder than necessary.

"Iron this for me, huh, Belly," he said. Daddy handed

Eve his shirt. Belly. He began calling Eve that when she was a baby—his way of distinguishing the girls' names. He'd never wanted them both named Eve, but Ma had insisted. When he tickled Eve Belinda on the tummy, he said her "belly button would smile." He started calling her Happy Belly, then just plain Belly.

Eve set the ironing board up near the sink. The kitchen was her favorite room in the house, because more than any other, it revealed the personality of each family member.

Her spot was wherever the ironing board stood. An old, faded report card, Al's from second grade, hung above the refrigerator. All A's. On the opposite wall, far above the twin portraits of Jesus and Dr. Martin Luther King, Jr., was an old, faded report card belonging to Ma. All A's, of course. Rows of grinning, smiling, bold, and shy photos framed the swinging door.

Fading time lines of Ma with her beautiful twin daughters, back when the girls were five, seven, and ten; back when grade-school boys called them the black, china dolls because of their dark, slanted eyes and deep ebony complexions.

"When do you leave again, Daddy?" Eve asked, stretching his shirt across the board.

"Gotta get the truck on the road by morning." His eyes shifted to the small television on the counter. The central plains lit up in somber shades as the TV voice explained the route of the upcoming storm.

"Belly?"

"I'll be done in a minute." His eyes reminded her of the time he had told her that Marilyn, the twins' dog, had been hit by a car. In a Polaroid on the wall, Eve and Al hugged Marilyn. They were in eighth grade, thirteen years old just like their dog. The photo was taken the day of Grandma Peaches' funeral. Staring at their identical outfits, Eve remembered it was the last time they'd dressed alike.

Eve returned her attention to Daddy's shirt.

"Al made a big mistake, Belly, but it's not the end of the world," Daddy said. "You don't have to make the same mistake, Belly. Hear me?

"Belly? Hear me?"

She nodded, her heart racing along with her thoughts. The way Daddy looked at her made Eve feel safe and loved, as if he could only see her as his sweet little girl. *Have mercy*, she thought. If he only knew what went on in her head when she thought of Lucious's behind in a tight pair of jeans—something she thought of often—or when she wondered what it would be like to hold him or have him caress her skin . . . or maybe more.

"Belly? Where are you at tonight, Baby?" Daddy was at her side.

The shirt made a sort of crinkling sound as she removed it from the ironing board. "Here," she said.

"Two months pregnant." Daddy was talking to himself, shaking his head. "My little girl is two months pregnant, and she won't even tell us who the father is."

Eve desperately searched her mind for a character, any character, she could play, whose lines were already written and spoken and tested, because she had no words of her own.

Daddy finished buttoning the shirt, thanked Eve for her help, then pulled her into a tight hug. The bell at the end of her red-and-white stocking cap tinkled. He whispered, "Belly, it was a mistake that Al made. Please, Belly, don't make the same mistake." Then he released her and disappeared through the swinging kitchen door.

I'll be the good one from now on, Daddy!

She wanted to make that promise, but deep down she didn't know if she could.

Act Two

Scene One

Scene One

No one called Mrs. Murphy Mrs. Murphy. "Call me Gloria," she insisted. Gloria believed students would like her more, think she was hip, if she let them call her by her first name. She was tall and thin, with yellowish-beige skin and spiky hair the color of dried blood. She didn't know that precisely an hour after they met her, the students in her 11:00 A.M. drama class nicknamed her Glow Worm.

"Glow Worm is in rare form today," Bethany whispered, opening her eyes wide to accentuate the thick swatch of blue eye shadow that made her look like a fairy godmother.

Eve whispered back, "Perhaps Madame should switch to decaf; she is definitely over-the-top today."

Bethany and Eve giggled. Bethany was Eve's best friend. Like most children born in Eden, Bethany had a name of "biblical proportions." That's how Eve referred to the not-so-subtle trend among town families to give their children names from the Bible. Up and down the rows of desks, from side to side and front to back, Eve counted multiple Marys and Josephs, a Jacob and a Matthew, two Fatimas, an assortment of Sarahs, and Rebekahs of numerous spellings.

Bethany thrust a folded scrap of paper toward Eve and looked both ways with the stealth of a spy.

"Ma hates Isaiah!" the note read.

"Why?" Eve silently mouthed the word.

Bethany rolled her eyes and shook her head. Glow Worm was on a tear at the opposite end of the room. They were free to whisper.

"She thinks we're doing . . . you know," Bethany said.

Eve knew. "It." Sadie Carmichael, Bethany's mom, had a lot in common with Eve's mom. They both had grown up in Eden. They both quoted scripture. And they both took themselves far too seriously.

They believed that their daughters were plotting the loss of their virginity the way Doppler radar plotted winter storms.

"No way!" Eve said.

"She is really starting to get on my last, last, last nerve."

"Starting?" The way Eve said *starting* sent both girls into spells of smothered laughter that attracted Glow Worm's attention.

Glow Worm stared at the two of them with such intensity, both girls slid down in their seats. Thrusting her fingers into her spiky, red hair, the teacher made a snorting sound, then continued her tirade across the room.

"That was close," Bethany whispered.

Eve sighed, absently touching the heart scratched into the wood grain of her desktop. Her fingertips traced the words *Johnny B. loves Ruth Ann.*

No matter how many times Eve sat at the desk, the carving always made her skin prickle.

When her mother, Ruth Ann, was a teen, everyone had thought she and Johnny B. would get married, but they didn't. When Johnny B. had returned to town a few months ago, Eden buzzed with *what ifs* and *might have beens.*

Eve sighed again, allowing her fingers to take another turn tracing the worn-down grooves in the desktop. She'd been assigned her seat on the first day of school. "Consider your seat assignments as your 'mark,' the place at which you will begin your discovery of self," Glow Worm had said. Eve looked at the carved name and thought about the significance of sitting at her mother's old desk—the very desk carved with the name of her mother's first true love.

Maybe Ma had been right. Maybe all the whispering about what might have been, all the gossip around town, had gotten to Eve. Maybe that's why she'd jumped to conclusions that night last April when her mother climbed into Johnny B.'s car and headed away from town. Ruth Ann had told Eve, Al, and Daddy that she was going to choir practice. But when Eve saw her get into Johnny B.'s car, she knew her mother wouldn't be going anywhere near their church or choir practice.

So Eve had called Aunt Mary. She had told her aunt that she'd seen her mother getting into Johnny B.'s car. She had said she wanted her aunt Mary to tell her something that would make sense. The truth was, all the while Eve had been talking to her aunt, Eve had felt the pounding of her heart, felt the watery wobble of her knees, felt the sheer, exquisite thrill of being a part of something . . . something a little dangerous.

She had been swept away by the notion of her mother running off with her first true love. So swept away, in fact, that she hadn't noticed her father come into the room while she was babbling to Aunt Mary.

One look into his dark, pained eyes, and Eve gulped. He turned on his heel and was out the door before she could form a word to stop him. The idea of her mother racing away with her old boyfriend suddenly made Eve sick to her stomach.

When everything got straightened out, Eve learned that Ma and Johnny B. had not been sneaking around in some sinful affair. Rather, Eden's onetime golden boy, Johnny B., had lost his career, his home, his money, and was on the verge of just giving up. Maybe even thinking about suicide. Eve's mother had taken him to speak with a preacher at another church. She was trying to prevent tongues from wagging. While Eve was suspecting her mother of infidelity, Ruth Ann was across the county in a preacher's office giving support to the man who'd broken her heart.

"Sssso," said Glow Worm, her hissy voice bringing Eve back from the painful past, "we have other matters of importance. You're all going to die, just die, die, die," Glow Worm said to the class. "You're all going to just die when you find out what play the drama department is doing for its spring production. Our spring production."

Glow Worm was practically shouting. Annoying as she was, Glow Worm was loved by her students, especially for her weirdness.

Glow Worm spun around and curtsied. Her thin arm flared out in front of her, a pale, willowy reed. Her head snapped upward with such force, several students recoiled.

Glow Worm was turning into a snake.

Using her bony hands, she beat her own drumroll on the dusty floor tiles.

"*The Crucible*. The fabulous, wondrous *Crucible* about

Puritans, obsession, and . . ."

Everyone in the room knew what was coming next. It was Glow Worm's most favorite of favorite words.

". . . and sex." When she said *sex*, it sounded like it had an *s* at the end. In fact, when Glow Worm got this worked up, a lot of her words had an extra *s* sound.

Finally Glow Worm announced that her students might have an opportunity to compete for summer-stock theater-group scholarships. At first her announcement was greeted with silence, then all the budding young actors, Eve and Bethany included, did just as Glow Worm had predicted. On perfect cue they all died right in their seats.

Glow Worm sprang from the floor, her wiry limbs stretching out like pipe cleaners. "See! I knew it! I knew you'd all just die! What wonderful, glorious, fabulous babies I have," she said, ending several words with her hissy *s*. Glow Worm walked up and down the aisles, surveying her dead students. Some were slumped forward, covering their desks. Others, as if impaled, held their arms back, their necks crooked to one side. Eve lay with her face plastered to the desk, one eye staring off into nothingness. Once again her chest pounded with excitement. Maybe this would be her big chance. She wanted that scholarship so much that it hurt. Glow Worm paused above her, nodding approval before continuing down the aisle.

Scene Two

Scene Two

Two class periods later, the dead had risen. Bethany joined Eve at lunch, picking up where she'd left off about Isaiah.

When Bethany tossed her head, thick, red curls bounced over her shoulders. "My mom bursts into my room accusing me of sneaking out of the house to have sex with Isaiah, and when she finds out I was actually helping Daddy set up for their stupid anniversary party, she says, 'It was a natural, honest mistake.' Natural! Ever since Isaiah and I started dating, it's like she doesn't trust me at all. Like I'm just skulking around, waiting for the right time for Isaiah to jump my bones or whatever else she thinks is 'natural.' Yuck! She really is gross."

"You'd think your mom would know about your germ thing, right?" Eve said, sipping from her milk carton.

Bethany, who was sipping homemade cider through

a straw she'd brought from home, sighed. "It's not like I'm totally crazy," she said.

"I know, I know," Eve said.

"But sex is quite germy," Bethany said. "You've seen those specials on The Learning Channel. If I were even thinking about having sex—which I'm not, thank you very much—Isaiah would need two condoms."

When she drew a breath, both girls looked at one another for half a second, then burst into giggles.

"You know you've got some issues, right?" Eve said, finishing her milk.

Bethany shrugged. Although she was a hopeless hypochondriac and obsessive about germs, it didn't stop her from being a pure romantic. She and Eve had dedicated hours, even weeks, of their friendship detailing, scripting, and directing their future love lives.

Bethany craved a *Shakespeare in Love* sort of first time, full of romance and surprise. Eve wanted more fireworks. Whenever they talked about it, Bethany would glance sideways at Eve and say, "You know you have issues, too, right?"

Eve had bought a video of *Armageddon* and had watched it, to date, thirty-three times. It was an action drama about a girl forbidden by her father to see the astronaut she loved—a man who would be called upon to help save Earth from a potentially life-ending meteor.

Or was it an asteroid? What was the difference between a meteor and an asteroid, anyway?

Bethany gave her a nudge. "You're thinking about *Armageddon* again, aren't you?"

Eve felt heat rise in her cheeks. Bethany shook her head gravely, "Issues. Iss-ues!"

They both laughed, but the laughter caught in Eve's throat.

Lucious Prior was standing just inside the door, talking to Principal Mann. Now, that had to be a sign, right? Sure, she'd seen glimpses of him around school since September. Word was that he helped out in the art studio. Still, for him to walk in right at that moment, well, what could it mean except that they were meant to be?

Automatically Eve squeezed her knees together. She wanted to stop the tingling that started in her belly button and raced down between her legs. Ma had told her, after that awful incident in April, that if "you weren't so preoccupied with sex, you wouldn't have jumped to such foolish conclusions about me and Jonathan." Ma was the only one who called Johnny B. Jonathan.

Bethany leaned forward. "Maybe you should talk to him."

Eve shook her head. For a moment, she longed to be back in middle school, where she'd established the pink-sweater-and-white-ribbon-wearing Good Girls

Club. The club members had passed out literature on abstinence and extolled the virtues of virtue. Several of the girls still got together to talk about alternatives to premarital sex. Back then she had faith that wanting to be good was good enough. But when she moved to high school and laid eyes on Lucious, she discovered sensations that boys in middle school had never inspired.

It was then that Eve began to hide from Mary B. and Mary K. and Fatima whenever they tried to include her in the club meetings, which they'd continued into high school. She hid until they finally gave up trying to include her.

Eve exhaled and dared a second look at Lucious. He had graduated last spring, but she still saw him around town a lot. Lucious and his artwork were legendary. He was a poet, a painter, a man with a soul. Not that tall, he was muscular. An ex-football player known for his sensitive art. How cool was that?

Known for getting barred from the graduation ceremony last spring. Known for the rumor that he was the father of Tracey Mayes's baby. In the yearbook he'd written: *Lucious Prior—nobody's daddy!*

The tingling in Eve's legs intensified as she thought back to the posters plastered around town last year.

The posters.

Scandal, pure scandal. Eve pictured the posters,

flashes popping in her memory. Lucious, his body perfectly chiseled, skin the color of sweet coffee with no cream, an assortment of tattoos glazing his muscles. Lucious, naked with his Eden Saints baseball cap barely covering his you know what.

Mmm, Lucious.

Looking over her shoulder, catching his eye one last time, Eve quickly turned away. Just looking at him made her whole body ache. Her whole body.

Scene Three

Daphne Rose gathered her long skirts around her ankles and dashed through the moonlit glen, her heart pounding beneath her bosom . . .

Eve could feel her own heart pounding, too, with each page.

"I knew you would come," said Dartanyan, his tall, muscular body filling up the night, blotting out the silvery moon. Despite the fact that Daphne Rose had been running hard enough for perspiration to dot her forehead, she shivered. Dartanyan loomed, a warrior ready to strike . . ."

A sound in the hallway broke Eve's trance. She let go of the book, and it dropped onto the braided rug by her bed. She lay silent. Waiting, waiting, waiting . . .

Nothing.

Eve swallowed a lump of stale air, then kicked the covers off her legs. Her body, much like Daphne Rose's, was moist with perspiration, her muscles taut like the strings on a harp.

Eve dangled her foot over the side of the bed. Carefully she stood up, hoping the aged, wooden floor would not moan. She leaned toward the shadeless lamp with its dim bulb and switched it off.

Outside, feathery snow shook from the sky. All of Eden lay beneath a white blanket. Eve stood at her window, releasing a great sigh. The whiteness stretched from Earth to heaven. Never ending.

Moving gently, careful not to make even the tiniest sound, Eve eased open the drawer of her nightstand. She took out a long, silver penlight that Daddy had given her. Eve plucked the book from the floor, slipped back into bed, and rolled onto her tummy. She began frantically skipping through the pages, past Daphne Rose's wild, midnight ride into the deserted glen, past Dartanyan's lumbering entrance. Page after page she skimmed by the dim glow of the penlight, pretending she was reading by candlelight hundreds of years ago as she burrowed beneath the covers.

Daphne Rose groaned with pleasure as Dartanyan lowered himself, careful of her fragile beauty . . .

What was it like to have sex?

Eve wanted to know so badly it frightened her. If she typed that question in an Internet search engine, what kind of answer would she get? Years ago Grandma Peaches had warned that sex was invented by Satan.

Grandma Peaches used to share lots of information about sex and sinners with her twin granddaughters. One thing was clear, good girls did not pursue sex.

Eve kept reading, her heart trembling against her nightgown, her legs too warm for the bedcovers, and by the time she reached the fateful page where Daphne Rose *released a quivering shudder of ecstasy*, Eve could almost do the same.

She crossed her feet at the ankles and used her muscles to squeeze her legs together with all her might.

Was something wrong with her? Ma would say it was sinful for a young lady to behave so. Heat seared her neck and face.

She rolled onto her back and slid her right hand under the covers and closed her eyes. Maybe it wouldn't be so bad if she just rubbed herself, you know, on top of her underwear. She bit her lip. She closed her eyes. Her fingers moved, slowly at first, then faster. Her breath caught in her throat. Guilt and anger worked against her like speed bumps blocking her air.

She promised herself each time that she'd never behave like that again.

What is the matter with me?

She rolled onto her side, sighed, lips quivering. Bad Eve, the Other Eve, was not ashamed of what she was doing. She liked it. Dared anyone to intrude.

The Good Eve, however, was terrified she'd get caught. She felt frustrated and confused. How she envied Daphne Rose.

Eve stood up and opened her bedroom door. She stared at Al's door across the hall. Was her twin sleeping? Was she thinking about the baby?

On an impulse, Eve knocked on Al's door.

"What?" a muffled voice called from the other side.

Eve stuck her head in. "Were you asleep?"

"What do you think?" Al said. She was leaning against a few pillows in the soft glow of her bedside lamp. A paperback was tucked inside a larger, hardcover book on her lap. Eve closed the door and moved closer to the bed, positive Al was reading a romance. But when she tried peeking, Al instantly slammed the larger book shut.

Al's walls were nearly bare. They were the color of fresh, farm eggshells, her ceiling cottony white. A framed certificate from the National Honor Society hung to the right of her bed, and books were stacked in all corners of the room.

"How're you feeling?" Eve asked. She sank into the cinnamon-colored chair at the foot of Al's bed.

"Why are you up so late? What are you up to?" Al asked, avoiding her question.

"I'm not up to anything," Eve said, a bit too quickly.

Everyone knew that Eve was always the first one in the house to fall asleep.

"So . . ."

"What?" Eve said.

"What do you want, Eve?" Al sat up straighter. She set aside the heavy book.

Eve's eyes went automatically to the thin, gold chain with the heart around Al's neck. Eve instinctively touched the identical necklace around her own throat. Gifts from their aunt Mary last Christmas.

"Eve? EVE!" Al repeated.

Eve took a deep breath and said, "I . . . I need to ask you something."

Al just looked at her.

"Uh, what was, you know, I mean, OK, what was . . ."

"Eve, stop babbling like an idiot. What's up with you? What do you want?"

"What was it like—sex, I mean?" The question came out of Eve in a rush.

Al didn't answer for a while. She just sat staring at Eve. "What do you want me to tell you, Eve? You want me to tell you that it's sweet and gentle and the best feeling in the whole world? You want me to tell you how he put his tongue in my mouth and licked my lips like I was the sweetest candy in the world? Huh, Eve, is that what you want me to tell you?"

"I . . ." Eve paused. Could she confide in Al that lately she'd begun to feel like a teen perv, always thinking about sex? Despite having been in the Good Girls Club, Eve had experienced her first real kiss in seventh grade. It hadn't sparked much in the way of desire, the way thoughts of Lucious did now.

Eve cleared her throat. "I just want you to tell me the truth."

"No you don't, Eve," Al said. She shifted, pulled her knees close to her chest, then stretched her legs out beneath the covers. Al's room was always cold, always. Even in the summertime. "You don't want to know the truth."

"I do. I mean, Al, sometimes it's all I think about. I feel like I'm going crazy. I don't have anyone to talk to about it. You know how Ma is," Eve said.

"Yeah." Al almost laughed. "I know how Ma is."

For a second the past hung between them.

Al and Eve had dreamed of a time when they'd run off together to Broadway and become big stars—Eve as an actress, Al as a playwright. They'd start out in the theater, then do movies, no, "film," and they'd appear on the cover of *Essence* and *Vogue* and *Black Enterprise* and *Entertainment Weekly* and on and on. This had been their dream.

But their big plans had had one huge obstacle: Ma.

Ma was determined that Al would go to law school. How else would Ma fulfill her dream?

So last spring, when Al was a junior, Al had confided her latest plan to Eve. Because she was going to graduate a year earlier than Eve, Al had applied for a year-long internship with a Detroit theater group. Her plan was to spend a year getting real-life experience while Eve finished her high school credits. Al would strike a bargain with their mother, saying she just wanted to take the year off to do something different before going to the University of Michigan for pre-law.

But she never planned to go to Michigan. Avoiding law school and pursuing a career in theater had been Al's secret plan.

Meanwhile Eve had laid plans of her own. While Al was applying for the internship, Eve had applied to the performing-arts high school across the lake, something their mother had forbidden.

As luck would have it, both girls' acceptances had come on the same day. Unfortunately Ma had intercepted the mail and had opened the letters. She had pounced on Eve when she came home from school that day.

"What do you mean, trying to get into a theater group?" Ma had misunderstood the letter. She had called Eve irresponsible and repeatedly snarled about how thickheaded Eve was and how she prayed all the time that Eve might one day be as sensible and rational as Al.

Eve was furious. Al this. Al that. Al was good. Eve was bad. Eve could not win. That was how she felt.

So Eve had blurted out, mostly to hurt her mother, "I didn't apply to that theater group; Al did." And to really twist the knife, she'd lied. Told her that the performing-arts high school was Al's backup plan.

Ma had exploded by the time poor, unsuspecting Al had walked through the door. Ma had been all over her, yelling about Al going behind her back and messing up her life. Al had felt blindsided and betrayed, and ever since that big drama scene, nothing had been right between the twins. Now they were having their first intimate conversation in months, and Eve's throat was dry and her stomach felt knotted up.

"I didn't say I wanted to have sex. I just wanted to, I don't know, maybe know what it would be like. I mean, I keep imagining myself in someone's arms, being held. Having him touch me and tell me that I'm beautiful and special. I just, I don't know, I want to feel connected to someone." Without thinking, Eve stood up while she was talking. She couldn't help it; whenever she thought of herself in love, she pictured herself in that scene in *Armageddon* in which the young astronaut and the girl are at a park, and the guy is gently tracing his finger along her bare belly.

Al threw her legs over the side of the bed. Her face was flat with anger and maybe even disgust. "You want to know what it's like, Eve? Really? I'll tell you then." She and her sister stood face-to-face. When one exhaled, the other breathed in. Their foreheads touched, and Eve imagined this was how they'd been in the womb.

Al clasped her fingers around Eve's arms and threw her down on the bed. "It starts off like this, Eve, with you on your back. I'll be the boy, Eve," Al said, flinging herself on top of her sister.

"You think you're in love, Eve," Al whispered in Eve's ear. "And that's not hard to do because he's whispering his *I-love-you*s in your ear. You want to believe him, so you believe him. Then he's touching you everywhere, and you're feeling everything everywhere all at once," Al said. Her hands ran up and down the sides of Eve's arms, rough and quick. Eve lay still, afraid to breathe.

"Then," Al whispered in Eve's ear, "you feel this awful pain between your legs and you hear lots of grunting. When he stops grunting, Eve, no one says I love you anymore. Then he gets up and you feel nasty and dirty, and that's pretty much that." Al pushed deeper into the mattress and stood up.

"So, Eve, is that what you wanted to know?"

Eve climbed out of the bed. She was sobbing. Her arms were wrapped around her body. "You're being awful and hateful, Al."

"Don't blame me. You said you wanted to know." Al didn't flinch. Each tear Eve shed seemed to fuel her anger.

"Is that what it was like for you? Were you raped? Is that why you won't tell anyone who the father is?" Eve was huffing and puffing, her face wet with tears.

"The father is none of your business," Al growled. Then almost in a whisper, she said, "Maybe being raped isn't the worst thing in the world. Maybe the worst thing is saying yes because you think you want to. Stupid . . ."

Eve rubbed her eyes with the backs of her hands. Al had, indeed, become a stranger. Eve felt a heaviness in her chest, and she thought she might gag. She was still gasping for air, fighting tears, when Al called out all singsong and bright, "Drop by anytime. Glad I could help."

Act Three

Scene One

Scene One

Eve called Aunt Mary and asked if she could go to church with her. Aunt Mary agreed to pick her up if Eve would help unload the boxes of books she was donating for a charity sale.

Aunt Mary stood in Eve's driveway, leaning on a gnarled, well-varnished, mahogany walking stick. Aunt Mary, with her meticulous Ebony Fashion Fair lipstick and tailored suits, often quipped that "mahogany and well varnished" could also describe her.

After they got in the car, Eve rode beside her aunt in silence. Absently she spun the radio dial and stopped at an old gospel song. Her foot started tap-tap-tapping against the floorboard of the big car. She was rocking gently in her seat, a flutter playing in her belly. Lately, whenever she rode with anyone other than her mother, she had this wild feeling she might throw the car door open and escape. Just run away. She was still picturing herself racing between the barren trees along mud-slicked foot trails when her aunt gave her a tiny nudge.

"We're here, Twin. Step lively. You've got books to unload!"

It didn't take long to unload the books. Afterwards Eve and her aunt went into the church and sat down for the morning service. Eve felt herself relax, inhaling the deep comfort of the familiar surroundings. Church felt safe, at least until the sermon.

" . . . if we think it, are we guilty of it same as if we had done the deed? Committed the sin? Let's talk about that . . ."

Eve gulped. How many times had Grandma Peaches smacked her arm or grabbed her ear and sneered, "Thinking sin ain't no different from doing sin. The good Lord will not tolerate whores in his kingdom!" Eve had been eleven the last time she had gotten the lecture. It had shaken her up so badly, she had been afraid that her love for SpongeBob would doom her.

Pastor Youngblood was talking, but Eve couldn't hear him, not with her soul rocketing straight toward hell. Aunt Mary reached over and squeezed Eve's fingers, unaware of her niece's one-way ticket to damnation.

Eve inadvertently thought of Lucious and the things he made her feel, the questions he left imprinted upon her. She knew she was way beyond SpongeBob now.

Could a person literally die from suffocation if the clouds in a small-town sky sank low enough?

Could a person, a pretty girl of around sixteen, lead two separate lives—one as a decent, honest, God-loving Christian; the other as a stark-raving sex fiend consumed with thoughts of doing you know what with you know who?

When the sermon ended, Eve's heart thumped a wild Congo rhythm. As Eve and Aunt Mary walked from the church, Eve's eyes darted back and forth across the walkway. She was anticipating Satan running up to take her away while Aunt Mary stared straight ahead, walking as upright as possible, considering her cane.

"Pastor Youngblood gave a good sermon today, wouldn't you say, Twin?" commented Aunt Mary.

Eve gulped. Thanks to the good words of Pastor Youngblood, she was more certain now than ever that she was full of sin.

She nodded, her voice too tight to speak.

Aunt Mary glanced at Eve. "Lord, help me, Twin, every time I look at you I think about how identical you girls are, yet so very, very different. Believe it or not, I see more of your mother's face in you than in Al. Even when Al and Ruth Ann chopped off their hair last summer, you still looked more like your mom. Maybe it's the softness around your eyes, I don't know, something.

That's it, I bet. The sweetness. That's Ruth Ann up and down. At least it used to be. It's still in there somewhere, I suppose."

Eve self-consciously tugged her soft, black ponytail. Last spring, after the big, April blowup, Al and her mother had gone off and gotten identical haircuts. Now both wore their hair in stylish pixie cuts above their ears. Eve had felt left out.

"Don't let Ma hear you say that. She hates me." Eve sighed.

"Nonsense!" Aunt Mary was walking slowly, using her gnarled, mahogany stick, and Eve slowed to keep the same pace.

"I wish all that mess from the spring had never happened."

"Ruth Ann doesn't hold any of that against you," Aunt Mary insisted. "You've got to stop beating yourself up and just embrace life, Twin. Be proud to be Eve."

Eve felt as if she'd been clubbed over the head. Standing on the sidewalk in the milky sunlight of winter, replaying the reverend's sermon and thinking about her own lust, it was not easy to think about being Eve. Who the hell was Eve, anyway? She didn't have a clue.

Proud to be Eve? Which Eve? The good, wholesome Eve everyone wanted her to be? The lust-filled, going-straight-to-hell Eve she turned into every time Lucious entered her thoughts, let alone the same room? The smart, wacky Eve her classmates saw when she showed up with her A papers and silly hats? The scared, frightened Eve who trembled in her own home, afraid she'd never win back the trust and love of her mother or sister? Or the Eve who sometimes threatened to overtake all the others—Angry Eve, the Eve who stared at the horizon and developed complicated schemes to get herself out of town, as far away as possible.

If Eve won that acting scholarship, she wouldn't have to scheme anymore. She could just be free. The fact that she couldn't discuss with her family how badly she wanted the scholarship made the muscles in her face tighten.

Aunt Mary clasped Eve's fingers. "Clear your mind, Twin. Ruth Ann loves you just as much as she loves Al, and Al is your sister and therefore loves you deeply, too. Just keep on thinking good thoughts like Pastor said, and keep a pure heart. Nothing can hurt you when your heart is pure, Twin. God won't let it."

Scene Two

Scene Two

Glow Worm swirled around the classroom, her vivid-green sweater hanging past her knees and clashing with her dirty-red hair color. Eve was only vaguely aware of her weird, wild teacher, since right now she was focused on *The Crucible*.

Ever since Glow Worm had announced it would be the big, spring production, Eve had read and re-read it. She would audition for the role of Elizabeth Proctor. Eve clutched the tattered text to her chest, feeling the words and doubts and fears of the pious woman who had risked everything for the man she loved. As she pictured herself in the world of puritanical Massachusetts during the Salem witch trials, Eve inhaled deeply.

"That's right!" Glow Worm said into her ear. Eve flinched. The teacher reached out and pointed one knobby finger at Eve's paperback.

"Miss Noble is holding the play against her heart. She is embracing it. Everybody, everybody who dares to dream about a role in the production, take out your play copies. Take them out and clutch them to your bodies. Do it now!"

Eve felt the color drain from her face. Bethany leaned across the aisle and whispered, "Glow Worm needs some sort of patch or a therapy group. Something to get her to calm down."

With the book still pressed against herself, Eve looked down to keep from giggling. When she glanced over, Bethany was looking at her copy as though it were a lover. She puckered her lips and made quiet, kissy noises.

"Smooch, smooch, smooch! Oh, how I love you, you big, hot, sexy play!" Bethany mouthed.

Glow Worm sprang across the room now, encouraging others to embrace the words of Arthur Miller as though they were the gospel. Eve shook her head at Bethany. "You are bad, bad, bad to the bone."

Bethany grinned. "That's right. Public enemy number one." Now they both laughed. Eve glanced down at her copy of *The Crucible*. She lightly drew her fingers across the well-worn cover, feeling every crevice and crease. She'd bought it at a used-book store in town. She wanted to get the role of Elizabeth. She had to have it.

If I can get that part, I can show that I deserve to be at the performing-arts high school, Eve told herself. When she closed her eyes, she saw her whole family, mother included, sitting in the audience, tears streaking their faces, elated to have someone so talented in the family.

The bell started ringing, and Eve's classmates rushed for the door as if there were a fire.

"So, you will audition, no?" Glow Worm spoke with a mock Italian accent. She tilted her head to one side, as if by doing so she would get her listener to realize she was using a foreign accent. By the time Eve was on her feet, book bag over her shoulder, the room had emptied.

"I really want to play Elizabeth Proctor," Eve said. She set a black, angora beret on her head, tucking her long, dark hair beneath the cap. Glow Worm stood beside her and threw an arm around her shoulder.

"Greatness! I can feel that you will bring greatness to the stage. I'm part psychic, you know." Glow Worm's eyes glistened, her prophecy bringing tears to her eyes.

Eve bit her lip. On an impulse, she threw her arms around Glow Worm and hugged her. When she pulled away, Eve felt dampness in her own eyes. "Getting this role means everything to me. Everything."

Glow Worm took another step back and gave Eve a solemn nod. "Before you attempt any role, it should absolutely command everything you have. Whether you get the role you seek or not, remember that your first commitment is to the work. Nothing else matters, Eve Noble, if you're not willing to do the hard, hard work."

Eve smiled. Glow Worm's face had a light sheen. She was putting on quite a show this afternoon. Eve felt honored. Not many students could lay claim to such private Glow Worm performances.

Eve pulled her shoulders back, pursed her lips, and, in her best imitation of a Puritan wife, said, "I plan to give it my all."

As she walked home, Eve thought about her promise to Glow Worm. She thought about the nearly weightless little paperback in her bag. She felt the knot of desperate need in her chest.

Once she showed her mother and Al how hard she was willing to work to be in the play and showed them that she was really and truly a great actress, they would forget their hard feelings. They would embrace her as she had embraced *The Crucible*.

She walked faster, her head bent against the cold air. Eve needed to believe it would work just like that, needed to believe that landing a juicy role in the play and doing a great job would make everyone proud of her and solve all of her problems. What else could she do?

Eve hunkered deeper into her winter coat and fought the wind and the doubt that threatened to knock her off her feet.

Scene Three

Scene Three

A few days later, when Eve arrived home from school, an unfamiliar car sat parked in the driveway behind Ma's car. Eve frowned. Why was her mother home so early from her paralegal job, and who was the visitor?

Eve sidestepped the slushy puddles of snow mixed with rain and pushed open the back door.

The kitchen was warm and smelled of fresh-brewed coffee and fresh-baked muffins. Not only was Ma home in the afternoon, but she was entertaining and baking, too.

Eve started toward the swinging door leading into the living room, but the loud, deep timbre of her father's voice made her freeze, one foot in front of the other, her entire body rooted to the floor.

". . . she's always been so bright . . ." Daddy boomed. He was laughing, a high-pitched, forced sort of laugh. What in the world was going on?

Eve pushed through the swinging door, took two steps into the living room, then froze again, the door clipping her on her shoulder. She didn't flinch. She just stared.

Ma stood instantly, clasping and unclasping her hands. "Eve!" Ma's voice was as high-pitched and strained as Daddy's. She wore an apron, an honest-to-goodness apron like the moms on those black-and-white sitcoms. Eve wondered whether or not she'd slipped into some sort of Twilight Zone.

On the sofa next to Ma, a man and woman sat side-by-side. The man wore thin, wire-framed glasses. The woman's face was hidden behind a coffee cup.

"Eve!" Ma chirped again. Ma almost never chirped. Ma was not a chirper. This had to be BIG. Eve watched, mesmerized as her mother waved her slender hand in the direction of the couple. She had all the grace and fanfare of one of Barker's Beauties on *The Price Is Right*. "Come over here, Eve, and meet the Mitchels."

The man and woman stood. Eve moved forward and noticed Al seated in the rocking chair. She hadn't even seen Al. Their eyes met briefly. Eve searched her sister's face for some sort of clue, but Al instantly looked down.

"Please, call me Lois," the woman said, looking from Ma to Eve. She extended her hand. "Eve? Nice to meet you," Lois continued.

Eve reached out and shook Lois's hand. "Hello, Mrs. Mitchel, uh, Lois."

"And I'm Charles," the man said.

"Please, Lois, Charles, sit; drink your coffee before it gets cold. The church sent the Mitchels to see Alexandra," Ma said. Although Lois and Charles took their seats, Ma held her game-show-hostess pose. Eve kept wondering whether her mother would announce that someone had just won a new oven. A trip to Paris. A camper.

Ma did none of those things. She cleared her throat. She touched her fingers lightly to the delicate gold chain around her slender throat. Ma's voice sang out in its chirpy, lighthearted, game-show tone. "Lois and Charles are considering adoption, and since Alexandra wants to put her . . ."

Then the gracious-hostess tone faltered and even Eve glanced away, feeling somehow embarrassed for her mother— her mother, who didn't know how to say with such bright resolve that the Mitchels were potentially there to take possession of Al's baby. When Eve glanced over, she saw Al squirm in the rocker.

So was this how it was going to be? Al was placing her baby up for adoption? Eve wanted to feel something, say it was right or wrong, feel it in her gut. But all she felt was fiery heat.

"WHAT LINE OF WORK ARE YOU IN AGAIN?" Daddy's voice shook the table. Eve glanced away from Al in time to see Lois Mitchel flinch and spill her coffee.

Ma sent Eve to the kitchen to get napkins and a towel. When Eve returned and helped blot up the spill, everyone seemed to be breathing normally again.

"Eve, it would be a tremendous help if you were to go downstairs and finish the load of laundry I started last night," Ma said.

Eve frowned at her mother. What load of laundry? Ma never did laundry.

"It's funny; you girls are identical, yet, there's something . . . I can't put my finger on it. You look just alike, but at the same time, you don't," Lois said. "Funny."

Eve glanced quickly at Al to see if she would snort, laugh, or say anything. Nothing. Al sat perfectly still, and Eve tried not to look down at her own breasts, for fear Lois Mitchel would stand and shout, "I know what the difference is. One of you is normal, and the other one has huge breasts like a stripper!"

"Excuse me," Eve said. "I'm going to go finish that laundry. It was nice meeting you."

Eve took the stairs two at a time. Sure enough, the dark, dank room underneath the living room was just as she'd left it a few days ago. Her mother hadn't been anywhere near the washing machine. Eve unzipped and peeled off her coat, dropping it to the floor. Then she heaved herself onto the dryer and sat with her ear as close to the vent as possible.

Charles Mitchel owned a business on the edge of town; Lois worked as an elementary-school teacher.

". . . mumble, mumble, mumble . . ." Eve couldn't make out much.

Al spoke only when spoken to, which was very much Al.

Yes, she planned to become an attorney. No, she'd never taken any kind of drugs. Yes, she wanted the baby in a decent home.

Eve made it out in bits and pieces, Al's voice disintegrating like snowflakes against a radiator as soon as the words reached the vent.

The soft murmurs continued, with Eve straining to hear until someone asked about the father.

"He won't be a problem," Al said, her voice now clear.

Charles wanted to know who the boy was; he wanted a name.

"He doesn't have a name," Al answered, her voice growing stronger.

Ma said something like, "Alexandra, he must have a name." Something about now being a good time to tell everybody who the boy was.

"I'll never tell you that. Never. If your adopting this baby depends on your meeting the father, forget it," Al shouted.

Al went on, ranting almost, about how the father nei-

ther used drugs nor was a felon or a criminal or anything like that. To her knowledge he didn't have any
handicaps in his family, and he didn't smoke or drink.
And most of all, "He wants nothing to do with this baby."

Al was crying.

Eve flinched and dabbed at her eyes. Once upon a
time they'd automatically cried together, but that hadn't
happened in a while. However, right now, Eve felt her
eyes itch and twitch.

Noise from above. All sorts of movement—chairs
sliding across the hardwood floor, Daddy's recliner
creaking on its hinges. The rattle of silverware against
the fancy silver tray.

Then footfalls, quick and heavy, right overhead, and
on the stairs. Al running out of the living room.

Eve hopped down from the dryer. Her knee bumped
a basket filled with poorly sewn squares of fabric. Ma
had tried her hand at quilting a few years back but
hadn't gotten very far.

Eve heard Ma apologizing for Al's rudeness. More
shifting around, the front door opening and closing,
then . . . silence.

*Pride goeth before destruction, and a haughty spirit
before a fall.*

Was it pride that kept Al's lips sealed, or did she have
something greater to hide?

"Were you eavesdropping?" Eve's mother met her at the top of the stairs. Eve shook her head.

"You didn't go running your mouth to Mary the other day, did you? The last thing I need is her two cents."

"I didn't tell her anything, although I don't understand what the big secret is. Eventually Aunt Mary is going to know."

Ma spun around. "She'll know when I'm ready for her to know."

"Ma, I want to help." Eve tried to smile, tried to look gung ho, as she followed her mother into the kitchen.

Her mother paused, rubbing her temples. Then she did something she hadn't done in months—she grabbed Eve by the hands and gently, but firmly, squeezed her fingers. "You know, you could do something for me. You could go through all those boxes of pictures you keep in your room and pick out some of you girls at different ages. If we're going to help your sister find a decent home for . . ." her voice faltered again.

Her eyes were shiny, her hands unsteady. "We have to help her. She isn't thinking clearly. You will help, won't you?" But she wasn't looking at Eve. She seemed barely to notice Eve's presence.

Eve's thoughts rattled around in her head. She nodded in response to her mother, then touched her mother's hand.

"It'll be all right. I'll help," Eve said.

When Ma looked at her, eyes shiny, brow furrowed, Eve experienced the sort of sensation that comes from taking a big drop on a roller coaster. Ma looked . . . scared. Eve didn't understand why, but seeing her mother's fear scared her, too.

Eve squeezed her mother's fingers and felt an electric thrill when her mother's fingers squeezed back.

OK, so now they were a team. They were working together. Maybe they could finally put the past aside. Faith, Eve told herself. Everything would be fine. She just needed faith.

As her mother walked away, Eve felt an odd mixture of giddiness and terror. She felt as if she were close to solving a difficult math problem and at the same time as if she were on top of a steep cliff, ready to jump.

Why?

Eve thought about the fear in her mother's eyes and tried unsuccessfully to blot out the image. Everybody was making plans and jumping through hoops on behalf of the one person no one would even acknowledge: Al's baby. Eve's niece. Ma and Daddy's grandchild. The baby none of them seemed to want.

Eve wondered, when her mother prayed at night, what did Ma pray for and what did she call the baby?

Act Four

Act Four

Eden stretched toward the heavens, wrapped in an icy, white blanket as far as Eve could see. The acting and dance workshop was coming to an end, and Eve stood next to Bethany looking out the third-story classroom window, their bodies glistening with sweat from an intense warm-up and stretch. With her leg on the bar, toes pointed and fingers reaching toward her toes, Eve saw something that made her stop.

Al?

"Are you all right?" Vivica—a girl whom Eve admired because she'd actually once run away to Los Angeles—arched her back and leaned forward to see what had stolen Eve's attention.

"I'm OK." Eve nodded, then moved as close to the window as possible to look across the street. Her twin was standing on the snowy sidewalk. Suddenly she snatched something from around her neck and threw it at a shadow in the doorway. What on earth was Al

doing over on this side of town when she was supposed to be at the library several blocks away?

The shadow reached out, and, for just a second, *it*
became *he*. A boy? A man? It was hard to tell. His body
stood at an angle, obscured from Eve's view. Eve shrank
away as she watched Al take a swing at him! Was Al in
trouble? Did she need help?

Before Eve could move her feet, Al raced up the block.
Seconds later the figure in the doorway came outside.
He was bundled underneath a huge coat and held his
face to one side, using his shoulder to block blowing
snow. He ran across the street and disappeared around
the corner.

"Who is that?" Vivica asked, but Eve didn't answer.
She grabbed her coat off the wall hook.

Bethany spun around. "Eve! What's up with you?
Where're you going?"

Buttoning her coat, Eve said hurriedly, "I just saw . . .
I mean, I've got to go."

Vivica came out of the coatroom with her own jacket.
"You look like you need company. I'm ready to blow this
joint, anyway," she said.

Who was Al throwing her necklace at?

Why was Al on this side of Eden in the first place?

Outside, Eve huddled inside her coat, her legs moving quickly across the street. She moved automatically

in the direction in which the man had gone. After she turned the corner, she felt Vivica grab her shoulder.

"Hey, wait a minute. What's your deal today? You look kinda freaked out."

Eve stopped, her eyes traveling up and down the block. Gray clouds sank low, their bellies full of snow. Empty streets stretched out, pale and gray in weak daylight. The shadowy stranger was gone, perhaps hiding in the belly of a cloud.

"My sister . . ." Eve began, then stopped herself. Al's condition was still very much a secret. "Never mind."

They walked in silence for a block or two. Downtown Eden was nearly deserted, even though it was Saturday afternoon. Eve tried to swallow, but a thick, sick feeling in her throat made it hard.

"You OK?" Vivica asked.

Eve nodded. Huge banks of snow crowded the intersections like gray, hulking beasts. Silhouettes of auto-manufacturing plants that had sat idle for a decade were etched against the feathery, winter sky. Tall smokestacks made Eve feel watched. She hated the vacated factories almost as much as she did the snow and the way everybody always talked about the weather.

"Are we looking for somebody?" Vivica asked.

Eve shrugged. "I guess not."

On the snow-packed sidewalk, their footsteps made

soft thumping sounds. "We should stop at the diner," Vivica said, her words puffing out in a veil of steam.

It took only a few minutes to reach the Eden Café. A tiny bell tinkled above the door when Vivica pushed it open. Both girls stopped to wipe their feet on the black, rubber mat.

"I'm not supposed to be working today, but it looks like ol' Nate could use some help," Vivica said.

Nate, the diner owner, waved from behind the fifties-style counter.

Vivica introduced Eve, and Nate shook her hand. "I know you. You and yo' daddy used to come in here all the time. Where is that old rascal these days?" He grinned, and Eve felt her face flush.

"Daddy's home," Eve said.

Nate nodded. "Yeah, that's right. Me and him, we used to work in the factory before it shut down. Well, I'm gonna keep an eye on you, 'specially if you done started running with this one," he said, pointing to Vivica.

Vivica wrinkled her nose at him and grabbed her apron. She headed to the back of the diner, where a group of guys was playing pool. Eve followed. Vivica was hugging someone. Although Eve's feet were moving, her body involuntarily halted.

BAM!

She was so startled, that it took a second to realize she'd walked into someone.

Arms, legs, winter coat, face . . .

Omigod!

The face. It was Lucious, and even though she'd taken a huge step back, he took a big step forward, leaving little room between them.

Scene Two

Scene Two

When Eve had walked into Lucious, he had played it cool, said it was his fault. He'd smiled at her, told her she'd hurt him. He pretended to double over with pain.

"You like the hats, huh?" he said, smooshing the crown of her black, velvet hat.

"They're my thing, you know? My signature. Hats are what I'm known for." Eve tried to sound so cool when she said it.

Lucious moved closer and dropped his voice to a whisper. "You're too pretty to be known for wearing silly hats."

When she met his gaze, Eve felt her hands tremble. She looked away, afraid he'd think she was some kind of weirdo. Then, just as quickly as he'd turned on the sexy vibes, he turned back to playful. "You gonna hang out here awhile?"

Eve gathered her composure, drew a slightly shaky breath. If she wanted to stay much longer, she'd need to call home. "Excuse me for a second, and I'll let you know," Eve said. She moved toward the phone and dialed. Daddy answered after two rings. She crossed her fingers, made her pitch, then exhaled. He gave her permission to hang out at the diner.

One hour turned into two, then into two again. Eve giggled self-consciously when Vivica put an apron on her to help with customers. No, it wasn't Vivica's shift, and, no, she wasn't supposed to be working, but, hey, the place was hopping and who couldn't use the tip money?

After a while, when the crowd thinned, Eve drifted to the tiny arcade area and accepted Lucious's challenge to one of the loud, beeping, bleeping games.

"I beat you again, Shorty," Lucious said. He was so close, Eve could smell his musky scent mixed with the sharp, sweet smell of turpentine. Had he been painting earlier?

"I don't play that often," Eve said. She stepped away from the video game and shoved one hand in her pocket.

"You probably just let me win," he said, grinning. "You're probably one of those arcade sharks setting me up so you can take my money."

Eve rolled her eyes, shoved him in the shoulder. "Yeah, right!"

He pushed back, still grinning. Lucious led her to a booth. They slid in and started talking.

Lucious said, "This time next year I plan to be in New York. That's where all the opportunity is if you're serious about being an artist."

Eve pictured herself running along the streets of great, big New York City, racing to an audition while Lucious raced toward a downtown gallery where his work was on display. He dreamed of moving to New York. She dreamed of moving to New York. It was fate. It was destiny.

Wouldn't they be perfect together?

Eve hadn't realized so much time had passed. Nate was sweeping. Vivica was at the end of the counter counting tips. Eve stood up and went to the counter. She took a damp cloth and wiped down several tables. She felt Lucious watching her, but she didn't dare turn around.

Is he looking at my butt?

When she finished, Lucious followed her to the coat hooks.

"You're a curvy little something, aren't you?" Lucious nodded toward Eve's sweater as she removed her coat from the wall hook. Quickly, she lifted her arms and protectively covered her breasts.

"I know you're not trying to flirt with my friend," Vivica said, shaking her hips and wagging her finger at Lucious.

"See, it's not even like that," Lucious said. His words came out slowly, in a drawl, but his eyes never left Eve. "I'm just saying she's got a cute shape, that's all." Lucious winked as Eve slipped into her coat.

"Whatever," said Vivica. She turned and grabbed her own coat, adding, "She's too young for you. And too good."

Eve opened her mouth to say something, then closed it again.

"She can look at me like the big brother she never had. How about that?" said Lucious.

Vivica snorted, "Boy, please. You're not hardly trying to be somebody's big brother. Like I said, she's too good for you."

They stepped outside into the frozen night air. The howling winds had died down. The air smelled good, crisp and wintry. A zillion stars jiggled against the sky.

Lucious was staring. Eve stood underneath the street lamp in front of the diner while Vivica stood beside her, stamping her feet to keep warm. Eve's father was on his way to pick her up.

"I'm outta here," Vivica said. She narrowed her eyes when she looked at Lucious. "And you behave."

He grinned and saluted. Eve said to Vivica, "Thanks. For everything, I mean. You know, leaving workshop with me, letting me hang out with you guys." Eve bit her lip, embarrassed. She sounded like a geek but didn't know how to shut up.

"No biggie, we had a good time, right? And you definitely earned yourself some tips—that's for real. Gimme some love, Lucious," Vivica said.

He pulled her into his arms and kissed her on the cheek. They were the same height, eye to eye. She looked over at Eve and said, "Keep your eye on him, and don't fall for that big-brother business."

Playfully he pushed her away. "See, why're you tripping, Vee?"

"'Cause I know you."

Lucious affected another military salute and said, "I'll be on my best behavior, Captain."

And maybe it was his best behavior. Lucious stood behind Eve, wrapped his arms around her, and pretended to try to throw her into the snow.

"You'd better not make me fall," she said, sounding brave, acting with all her might. The screen in her head went fuzzy. What movie? What sound track? What did being here, right now, remind her of? Characters and dialogue flipped around so fast, yet nothing stuck.

"You couldn't stop me if you wanted to," he said. Then he got close, real close, his lips brushing the side of her neck, a spot that had been made cold by the night air but now, with him right there, right on it, felt warm, and the tingles went directly from her neck to her heart.

"Do you want me to stop?" he whispered.

Eve started to whimper.

"Do you want me to stop?" he repeated. He pulled tighter.

She shook her head, afraid to say anything because she didn't know if she could speak. His lips brushed her there again, then again.

Dull and sparkling at the same time, headlights rolled across the icy ground, bouncing off the diner's front window. Twin yellow spotlights shone on Lucious and Eve.

He released her, then whispered, "I'm just playing around with you, girl. Just having some fun."

She nodded, trembling.

He said, "You should let me sketch you sometime."

She ran to her father's car, waving over her shoulder but afraid to look back. How could she describe the way she felt? In all the times that she'd imagined herself actually talking to Lucious Prior, never in a million years had she believed hanging out with him for real could feel so good.

Music from the radio—the blues, good, old-fashioned blues—blared and filled the car. "Have a good time tonight, Belly?" her father asked, turning the volume down as the car crunched along the ice.

Eve held her breath, not wanting to meet her father's gaze. The same feeling that had gripped her in the kitchen the first night she and her father talked about Al's being pregnant, the oily feeling that had wedged in her stomach, came back. She could feel him watching her, could hear the unstated implications of his question.

As soon as Eve glanced at her father, she knew her fears had been right. She saw it in his eyes. Saw the pain that came with wanting to make sure she wouldn't make the same mistake Al had made.

"We had fun tonight, Daddy!" Eve said, quickly. She knew her voice was too high, too bright.

Her father glanced at the rear-view mirror. His gaze lingered for a few seconds, then he nodded his head back toward the diner. "That boy back there, do I know him? Was he . . . is he a friend of yours?"

Eve prayed he wouldn't turn on the interior lights, because, if he did, he'd see the color rising in her face. Blessedly, the only light inside the car came from streetlamps fogged over with crusts of ice and the occasional dump truck leaving trails of salt to melt the snow.

"He's nobody, really. Just a boy that Vivica knows," Eve said.

Her father kept his eyes on the road. His large hands

gripped the steering wheel. He gave a barely visible nod. A fine mist of steam encircled his face as he lightly sang the blues.

If Eve didn't know her father better, she'd think he was downright chipper. But she did know him. And she knew he was scared. She wanted to tell him how connected she felt to Lucious, how, even though this was the first time they'd spent any real time together, she was convinced he was her soul mate. She wished she could tell him how confused it all made her feel, how scared and happy and sick and delighted she got just thinking about the boy. If she could tell him all of that, she thought, maybe he wouldn't worry so much.

But it wasn't the right time. Her father loved her, but he didn't want to know about her being all gaga over some boy. Not now.

For now, Eve thought, what she felt for Lucious would just have to remain her secret.

Scene Three

In the kitchen Eve finished her glass of milk and headed toward the living room. For a moment she paused. A feeling . . . something was . . .

"Ma!"

Her mother was standing less than a foot behind her. When had she come in?

"Think you're slick, don't you?" her mother said, her voice low, same as Lucious's, but the heat she gave off was totally different.

Eve was too stunned to move, too shocked to act.

"Calling your father and getting his permission to hang out with that little tramp so you could sidle up to all kinds of boys," her mother said, grabbing her arm.

"I didn't," Eve said. But, awful as it sounded, wasn't her mother right? Hadn't Eve known that if her father answered the phone he'd let her stay at the diner, whereas her mother would have ordered her home?

Hadn't she wanted to hang out so she could be close to Lucious? *Sidle up* sounded extra sinful.

Her mother released her grip on Eve's arm, and her voice cracked. "It's bad enough I've been made a fool of once . . ." Her voice trailed off. Ruth Ann Noble bit deep into the flesh of her top lip, obviously to fight back tears. "Please, Eve. I don't know how we're going to get through this thing with Al. Please don't make me worry about you, too. Please!"

"I won't do anything bad, Ma," Eve said, her voice young and helpless.

Her mother took a step back. "I'm counting on you, Eve. Counting on you to keep your word." She inhaled deeply, then left the kitchen.

In her room Eve knelt down beside her bed. Her mother's plea felt like a burn, but remembering where Lucious had touched her with his lips and maybe even his tongue . . . Oh, Lord, she needed forgiveness, guidance, something.

"Our father, who art in heaven . . ."

Eve prayed that night, prayed and prayed and prayed.

She prayed God would help her find her way, because right now, she couldn't feel more lost.

". . . Amen."

"Is Al a virgin?" Benny asked.

"What's a virgin?" said Nick, stirring clumps of gooey cereal.

Ma was babysitting again for Eugenia's boys. Nick and Benny were going to be in the school Christmas pageant. After Al had torn out of the kitchen earlier, racing for the bathroom to throw up, Ma had explained that Al was sick because she was going to have a baby.

"Hush up! Hush your mouths," Ma said. "Mary in the Bible is the only virgin you need to worry yourselves with."

"Well, is she? Eve, is Al a virgin?" Benny slid off the high stool and clunked his bowl in the sink.

"Virgin, wergin, sturgin," Nick said over and over, adding the evil laugh he had learned from cartoon bad guys. He was four; Benny was six.

Eve held her body erect, the dog-eared copy of *The Crucible* in one hand, a cup of lukewarm coffee in the other. Tryouts were a few days away. She glanced over her shoulder at Ma, who was wringing her hands and chewing her lip. Hand wringing and lip chewing at breakfast were not good signs.

"Is Al a virgin?" repeated Benny.

"Virgin, sturgin, burgin," said Nick.

"Enough, you two. Now get your things and get ready for school." Ma hid her face in the refrigerator.

Benny said, "But in the Christmas pageant, the Virgin Mary is having a baby. So is Al a virgin like Mary?"

"Hell, no," Al said from the doorway, eyebrows arched, her hand pressing against the middle of her back as though she were already months and months along.

Eve pulled her shoulders straight. ". . . *And that's an upright answer,*" she said, reading one of Elizabeth's lines.

"You watch your mouth, Miss Missy," Ma scolded Al, then threw a quick frown at Eve.

"I am not a virgin, Benny, and if you ask me, neither was Mary." Al eased into a kitchen chair. "Joseph, Mary's husband, would have ditched her if the angels hadn't begged him to stay. He didn't believe she was a virgin, either."

Eve's eyes continued to scan the dialogue. Ma's fuse had been short and was getting shorter by the day.

Eve glanced at *The Crucible* pages, swept her arm wide, and held her body the way she believed an angry, upright woman in the eighteenth century might. Elizabeth's question regarding dear friend and accused witch, Sara Good, tripped from her tongue: *"Pregnant! Are they mad? The woman's near to sixty!"*

"Quiet, Eve." Ma scowled. She turned back to Benny. "Get moving!"

Benny grabbed Nick as the younger boy repeated, "Wergin, sturgin, virgin, mergin, turgin . . ."

Ma rocked from side to side, a nervous habit she had, as she watched the boys race from the kitchen. "If Mama Peaches were alive, Lord have mercy, I can't imagine what she'd say!"

Instinctively Eve glanced at Al. The two clenched their jaws in unison, both bracing for the familiar tirade. Since Grandma Peaches's death, Ma had considered their grandmother the final authority on child rearing.

"Mama thought if I kept you two independent and pushed you in your own directions, it would make you both stronger," Ma muttered, wringing her hands. "Didn't work, didn't work, didn't work . . ."

"Oh, please!" Al snapped.

That got Ma's attention. She rushed over to Al and slapped her palm on the table so hard, the sugar bowl rattled and the silverware jumped. Eve flinched; Al didn't. Al and Ma were face to face, but unspoken anger pushed them miles apart.

"Don't you ever bring your trashy mouth full of blasphemy in front of Eugenia's boys again. Hear me? And show me more respect, too, thank you very much!" Her outburst caught Al off guard. Eve, too.

Ma was rocking again, the way she did in her Sunday girdle, not that she needed a girdle. Al and Eve had once joked a few years back that the only reason Ma wore a girdle was so it would keep her all bound up. That way she'd be able to more easily mimic Grandma Peaches.

Eve understood why half the town once regarded Ruth Ann as some sort of princess when she was young. Eve had seen the pictures. Her mother had been beautiful then, and she was beautiful now.

"I was answering his question," Al said.

"You were being trashy," Ma said. Then she brought her hands to her face and wiped away huge tears. Eve wondered how she did it. How she made such huge, sad, wonderful tears so quickly. Perhaps Ma kept lots of pain stored up, saving it for the right time to roll down her cheeks. Elizabeth Proctor, accused witch and good wife, cried often. If Eve got the role, she prayed that she, too, could cry great, glorious, round tears, same as Ma.

"When you're bad-mouthing Mary, you need to be on your knees somewhere praying. And remember this, when Mary delivered, her baby had a father. You can't say the same, now, can you?"

The Crucible made a soft thump against the floor when it slipped from Eve's hand. Neither Ma nor Al noticed.

"Well, if and when I do marry, at least I'll marry someone who . . ."

Too far . . . too far . . . too far . . .

Eve knew where her sister was going. Accusing her mother of settling for Daddy because she couldn't have Johnny B. Well, this was a bad time to bring that up.

"Al!" Eve cut in. Should she dance? Drop dishes? Juggle fruit? Should she do something—anything to change the subject?

"What, Alexandra? What are you saying?" Ma stepped closer.

"*There's no business like show business . . .*" Eve began to sing. An emergency show tune. Her mother, smoldering and puffing and brimming with heat, paused.

"Stop that damned nonsense," Ma shouted. Eve went down on one knee to signal her big finish, and by that point both Ma and Al appeared out of steam. Ma muttered something, then stalked out.

Eve was shocked to see that Al was close to tears.

"Are you all right?" Eve asked.

Al slumped forward, her face in her hands. "I hate this!"

"What? Being pregnant?"

"Maybe I should have told Benny that *you* are the family virgin."

"Are you trying to provoke me like you were provoking Ma?" Eve used her best Oprah, I'm-every-woman's-best-friend voice and said, "I can help you, Al. I want to help if you'd just let me."

Al took a bite of the leftover toast on Benny's plate and brushed away the crumbs. "You're a regular angel. Possibly a saint. Like I said, maybe I should have told Benny you're the family virgin."

"I would be afraid for my soul, if I were you," Eve said, making her voice sound low and grave as she bent to pick up *The Crucible*.

"Don't worry about my soul, Virgin Eve. At least, I think you're still a virgin. Who knows what you've been doing with Lucious Prior, the way you've been making eyes at him."

Eve grasped the front of her white collar, then pressed her fingers against her heart as though she feared she would pass out.

"I have done nothing with Lucious Prior! Why do you accuse me so?" Yes! That was precisely how Elizabeth Proctor, good woman, good Puritan, would say it.

"Stop acting! You make me sick with all your acting." Al gritted her teeth. "You're not even serious about it. It's just a game to you. Everything is a play to you!"

"All the world's a stage, and all the men and women merely . . ."

"Shut up!" Al yelled. Then, drawing a deep breath to regain her composure, Al smiled. When she spoke, her tone was almost sweet. "Come to think of it, maybe that's really how those things got to be so big," she said, pointing to Eve's breasts. "Maybe you're not the only one touching them, making them grow. Has Lucious been helping you?"

Eve crossed her arms over her chest, backing away. "Why are your thoughts so . . . so impure, Al? Why?"

"Well, Virgin Eve, I'll bet I'm not the only one in this room with impure thoughts."

Bulls-eye!

"Lucious Prior has an impure reputation, too," Al continued. "But with him you don't seem to mind so much, huh?"

Eve didn't want to trade shots any longer. Clearing the table, she said, "He barely even knows I'm alive."

"Oh, he knows, Virgin Eve. He knows."

Scene Five

So much pretense. The brightly decorated, cardboard fireplace leftover from the Christmas pageant became an ancient hearth. The stage became a cement floor, and other pageant remnants became meager belongings in a Puritan couple's home.

"Once more, this is our last time," said Glow Worm, snapping her fingers. "Quiet, people. Callback tryouts to cast the role of Elizabeth Proctor for *The Crucible*, Act II."

On cue Eve began to hum as Erick Ross entered the stage. Erick was pretty much a shoo-in for the part of John Proctor. After three days of tryouts, Eve was one of the finalists auditioning to play the coveted role of John Proctor's wife, Elizabeth.

"*What keeps you so late? It's almost dark,*" Eve read from her book.

"*I were planting far out to the forest edge,*" Erick said. His copy of Arthur Miller's drama was shoved in his back pocket. He was a senior and a veteran of the drama club.

"*Oh, you're done then,*" Eve read, glancing up.

"Stop, stop, stop!" Joel Cryer, the director, called out.

Glow Worm wiggled in her seat and ran her fingers through her spiked hair. Joel smiled at Eve and said, "Eve, you're doing fine, but I need you to relax. Remember, you're John's wife. You don't have to be so shy with him."

Eve nodded and began again. By the end the scene felt good. Erick held her hand, squeezed her fingers reassuringly. Or was John merely comforting his wife?

After the tryout Eve lingered on the stage. Her mother had been crowned homecoming queen in this room. On this stage Johnny B. had been king. A cheerleader and a star quarterback. While Al had always thought the stories of her mother's high school popularity were clichéd and sad, Eve found them tremendously romantic.

"Hey, how's Al?" Erick slapped Eve on the back, knocking her into the present. She gasped.

"Sorry," Erick said. "Didn't mean to startle you."

"What did you ask me?" she said.

"Al. I asked how's she doing. She spends half her day over at Community taking college courses. I never see her anymore."

"She's OK, I guess. I mean, she's OK," Eve mumbled. She put her hands on her hips and eyed him directly. "Why do you want to know?"

"No reason. Dang," Erick said, his face turning bright red. "We're kind of like friends, you know, whatever. Anyway, tell her I asked about her. Tell her I said good luck, you know, with everything."

Eve stared for a moment, suddenly remembering that Erick and Al had worked together during the summer and that Erick had been one of the few guys that Al had not made fun of. She actually came home one time and said that Erick was pretty smart, for a guy. High praise for her.

Could Erick be the father of Al's baby?

"Announcement, announcement. Gather round, my darlings." Glow Worm's voice cut through Eve's thoughts. Eve glanced around, her eyes resting momentarily on Molly Horn and Amanda Woods, her competition for the role of Elizabeth Proctor.

"First, let me say that all of you have been wonderful dears," Glow Worm said. "We will post our final cast list in the morning. Second, let me remind all of you that even though rehearsals will not start in earnest until after the holiday break, we want you to take our spring production very seriously. April may sound like a lifetime from now, but it is staring at us from around the next corner." Glow Worm paused, using her hand as a visor for special effect.

"I know I should wait to tell you, but I can't, I can't, I can't; it's too juicy," Glow Worm continued, adding several extra *s* sounds. "Those of you fortunate enough to earn parts in the play will not only have the opportunity to hone your acting skills under the fine direction of Joel Cryer, but you'll also be competing for the three available scholarships to summer-theater group. In NEW YORK CITY," she said, practically bouncing off the ceiling. Gasps and cries rained like confetti, and Eve felt herself floating away.

The next morning Eve's fingers laced with Bethany's as the two charged into the school to read the final cast list.

Bethany was thrilled to discover that she'd landed the role of Mary Warren. She gripped Eve's arm as Eve drew in one last deep breath. Eve couldn't speak as she read the final cast list: "Elizabeth Proctor—Amanda Woods."

Eve stood silent. Her lips trembled and fat tears spilled from her eyes. Bethany hesitated a moment, then gathered Eve into her arms and hugged her.

The next day was Christmas Eve. School had let out for Christmas break, and Eve was fidgeting around in the kitchen, still stung from losing the role she had so wanted.

Daddy stepped into the kitchen. "Belly!" he cried. Then he stopped and laughed, since Eve, to cheer herself up, had dressed as a court jester. Daddy reached over and jingled the gold bell dangling from the tip of her red-and-white stocking cap.

"Daddy, hey," Eve said. Jingle-jingle went the tiny bell as her father squeezed her in a hug.

"Where's everybody?" Daddy asked.

"Ma took Al to the doctor for her appointment. Right now looks like it's just me and you," Eve said.

"I don't suppose you want to tell me about that getup you're wearing," Daddy said, going to the refrigerator. Eve turned her palms upward to fully display her court-jester appearance.

"Let's just say I was feeling a little bit like a fool today." She sighed.

Daddy shook his head. "Maybe lunch and some last-minute shopping will make you feel better."

Eve whipped around, making the tiny bell on her hat tinkle. Theatrically she took a deep bow, gestured toward her father's feet, and said, "I'm at your service, sire."

An hour later they were sitting in a booth near the

window of the Eden Café. Eve sank down against the vinyl cushion and let out a dramatic sigh. "I didn't get it, the part, I mean."

"Oh, Belly, I sure am sorry." After a pause Daddy added, "You know, I never did believe those folks at your school had much good sense. Now I know it." Like always, Eve found it impossible to stay sad with her father around.

After lunch Eve did some last-minute gift shopping with Daddy, then returned home to find Ma's car parked out front and Al at the kitchen table.

Al didn't look up when they came in, but she mumbled in Eve's general direction, "There's a message for you, Eve."

Eve snatched the note off the counter and ran upstairs for some privacy. She wasn't even sure she was breathing as she punched in the numbers.

"Joel?" Eve's voice was tentative.

"Eve! Great news. We know you tried out for the role of Elizabeth Proctor, but some of us have talked it over and we'd really like to see you as Abigail Williams. Do you think you're up for it?"

Her mind went blank. Eve couldn't speak—a true first for her.

"Eve. Eve? You still there?" the voice said into her ear.

"Uh-huh," Eve breathed.

"And . . ."

The one-word answer started in the tips of her shoes and moved through her body. Jumping up and down, up and down, Eve shrieked, "Yes, yes, yes, yes, yes, yes. . . ."

Eve Noble was going to star in *The Crucible* after all.

Act Five

Scene One

On Christmas Day at Aunt Mary's farmhouse, Eve kept her secret folded neatly against her heart. Throughout the afternoon, as cousins and aunts and uncles shared stories and songs, Eve chewed on her lip and wondered if the time was right to share her wonderful news.

Eve felt the presence of the *other secret* as though it were a guest unseen. It was still too early for Al's pregnancy to really show, and, as far as Ma was concerned, Aunt Mary was not to find out. Not yet, anyway.

So Aunt Mary was in the dark about the sudden, ashen expression on Al and Ma's faces when she introduced her friends Tom and Cally Shepherd. Aunt Mary's new neighbors were a husband-and-wife veterinarian team, and they were proud of Cally's perfectly round, six-months-pregnant belly. Eve tried to hide her amusement as she watched Ma's face tighten as if she'd overdosed on BOTOX.

After Tom started talking about horses, Eve accompanied him to the stable and helped him feed and brush the horses, five in all. She took extra time with Strawberry, her favorite, the one she'd ridden most often.

When almost everyone was gone, Eve sat in Aunt Mary's huge kitchen while Ma stacked dishes at the sink. Al stood behind Eve's chair, her fingers expertly lacing Eve's hair into delicate sections, one after another, weaving them into glossy braids. On the ride from town, Al had said that after wearing so many stupid hats, Eve's head looked like the back of the Christmas manger. Then she said she'd braid it. Eve wanted to believe that Al's offer was a gesture of forgiveness. But she knew better. Aunt Mary made Al nervous, and braiding Eve's hair would help Al relax.

"Twin, you do a most fabulous job," Aunt Mary said in her low voice as she brewed coffee. "The relationship between twins is a special one, girls, so cherish it. What I wouldn't give to have my own twin, Myra, standing next to me." She slipped her arm around Ma's shoulder, a tear resting on one high cheekbone. Ma's face went soft, and her eyes became distant. Aunt Mary and her twin, Myra, had been twelve years older than Ma, but Myra had died of pneumonia when Ma was still a toddler.

With a flourish Aunt Mary drew Ma closer, squeezed, then let go and looked at Al. "Oh, my Ally-Ally, how wonderful it is that you will be off to college come summer. I am so very, very proud, and I know your Grandma Peaches would be proud, too, God rest her living soul."

Al's fingers paused mid-braid, and Eve felt the air go still. When Eve twisted her head around, her eyes locked with Al's. In an instant Eve understood what Al must be thinking. All this pride, all this praise, yet she was three months pregnant, sixteen, and wanting to get out of her small-town life. But Al had to fulfill the legacy of a high-achieving aunt.

"Look down," Al commanded. The connection was broken. Eve turned her head, and Al finished the braid.

Aunt Mary came closer. "I spent thirty years of my life building a career as an attorney," she said in a level voice. "You won't have to face the same challenges I did at a time when black, female professionals were still being measured in 'firsts.' Mama Peaches helped me make it with money from her bakery."

"Done," Al said, releasing Eve's hair and giving her shoulder a push. Eve surveyed her new do in the mirror beside the sink. She took a deep breath. It was time, she thought. She would share her good, good news.

When Eve stepped forward, her mother said, "Al is

going to be just fine, and I've got a nice surprise for Eve, too." Eve paused, caught off guard. What was going on?

Ma smiled at Aunt Mary and said, "I fixed it so Eve can work part-time at Franklin and Stein . . . with me." She cleared her throat. "It'll just be after school a few days a week, but Eve'll be able to get some good, secretarial training, make some money, help out. We're going to need all the money we can get when Al goes off to school next fall, not that Eve's money would go to Al. But this way, Eve'll have her own spending money and get more exposure to a reasonable line of work." Ma's voice was as bright and shiny as the holiday lights.

A moan escaped from Eve's throat.

"No, Ma, I can't!" she wailed.

Everyone turned to stare at Eve. She wanted to hide. This was not how Eve had wanted to share her good news.

"I was just going to tell you, I got the part. A part, I mean. In *The Crucible*. I could win a scholarship to summer-theater group. Rehearsals are going to take up a lot of my after-school time."

For a moment, there was silence. Then Ma said, "We've been through this before, Eve. I'm not letting you get up onstage and shame yourself, or this family, shaking your behind and carrying on."

"Oh, Sweet Pea, listen to yourself," Aunt Mary cut in, her normally steady voice rising an octave. "You sound all the world like Mama Peaches."

"But . . ." Ma began.

"But nothing, Sweet Pea. Now, lest we forget, I spent time on the stage, too," Aunt Mary boomed. "Miss Ruby Dee might have made the role famous, but I did a mighty-fine turn as the wife in Lorraine Hansberry's *A Raisin in the Sun*. You know, they suggest drama courses for lawyers, say it helps us in the courtroom."

"But Eve wouldn't even consider going to law school like Al or you, Mary." Ma grimaced.

"Well, dearest, you just said you got her a part-time job in your law office. I'm just reminding you that the theater offers fine things to young people. So let's think on this. Last time I checked, *The Crucible* didn't have much butt shaking. I think it's wonderful that Twin is so passionate about life."

"Mary, I know you studied drama," Ma began, coming around the kitchen island. "I know how good you were onstage. And Eve . . . she's very bright, but she's, she's . . . frivolous."

Eve felt an incredible weight on her chest. A pressing, crushing feeling that pressed from her scalp to her cinnamon-red-painted toenails.

"You can't mean it, Ma," Eve rasped in a whisper.

"Eve, don't tell me my mind," Ma said. "See what I mean, Aunt Mary? She's high-strung and always has her head in the clouds. I know Al is going to be a lawyer someday, just like you. But Eve, if I don't watch out for her, there's no telling what she's liable to get herself into."

Ma was picking up steam. "I know you *think* you want to be an actress, but when you play around so much, how can you really know? I just want the best for the real Eve, not some fantasy you've cooked up."

Ah, yes. The real Eve. As real as Mommy will let her be!

"But Ma, when Al used to write plays and I'd star in them, you didn't seem to mind so much. Why is it so wrong now?"

"See? You don't even know the difference between child's play and real life. It's always something with you, Eve, and now it's acting. And then there's all your boy craziness. Been trying to have a boyfriend since you were in preschool. You just don't focus, Eve."

"Ma, I'm almost a straight-A student. Just because I didn't skip a grade like Al doesn't mean I'm drooling on my collar while I wait for the bus for 'special' kids."

"Leave my name out of it, please," Al said, putting away the hair supplies she'd used to style Eve's hair.

Eve turned to her sister. Clenching and unclenching

her fists, Eve paced. She couldn't breathe. *Lord, what is it going to take for you to cut me a break?*

"I wish I could leave you out, but I can't, can I? Not when everything always comes back to you. Al plans to go to college. Al gets all A's. Al's going to have a bright future. Then Al goes off and makes a big mistake, and the next thing you know, we've got to rein in Eve before she makes the same mistake." The words shot out of Eve with such force, Al flinched.

"This isn't my fault. I don't care if you're in a stupid play or not," Al said, lips tight and eyes narrow.

"No, you don't care about anything but Al. This *is* your fault. You did this. You got in trouble, and now Ma is taking it out on me, making me work with her so she can keep her eye on me."

"What accident? What mistake?" Aunt Mary asked.

Eve, Ma, and Al turned to Aunt Mary. Eve's mouth opened, then closed.

"Now, look what you've done," Ma said. Eve felt a shiver. She knew her aunt was not supposed to find out about Al, certainly not like this.

"Look what I've done?" Eve felt the blood drain from her face.

"Tell me, Al, what's this about? Are you in some kind of trouble?" Aunt Mary leaned on her cane, walking toward Al.

KENNEDY

Eve felt light-headed. Had she really made the same mistake again? Betraying Al and her mother to Aunt Mary?

"Eve, I really thought you would buckle down and try to make things better at a time like this." Ma shook her head. "Well, I can't see the good sense in letting you be in some play. Not now!"

"Sweet Pea, let her be! Now, what's this about Al?" Aunt Mary demanded. Eve edged backward. She grabbed her coat off the wall hook. "I have to be in that play, Ma. I have to."

"Look at all the trouble you've caused with your selfishness," Ma said.

"I'm sorry, Ma. I didn't mean to. . . . It slipped out."

"Just like you didn't mean to tell James about seeing me with Johnny B., eh? You seem to have a knack for slipups that'll hurt me." Ma's face was stone.

"Sweet Pea! Get control of yourself!"

Eve edged toward the back door. She had to get away. She flung open the door and rushed into the ice-cold air.

Her feet moved, crunched in the wet snow. *Faster.*

She was running, coat flapping in the wind. She reached the stable, huffing and puffing.

Now the tears.

Thick, fat splashes, salty and bitter.

Ma was so mad now, Eve didn't stand a chance of being in that play. She grabbed Strawberry's brush and briskly stroked it against the horse's reddish coat.

"Eve!" a voice called to her. But Eve didn't stop to figure out who was calling her name. She couldn't take it. Couldn't take another minute of her mother's praising Al while looking down her nose at her.

Once the horse's bridle was in place, Eve didn't wait to place a saddle on her back. She mounted the horse bareback, squeezed her thighs, and the animal moved forward. Thick, frosty air tore apart like icy fabric as Eve urged Strawberry into a full run. Her lip trembled. She urged Strawberry to go faster. Al could get away with whatever she wanted. Al could do whatever she wanted and be whatever she chose. Everybody knew who Al was. Al was a real person, unlike Eve, who had her "head in the clouds."

"What about me, Ma? Huh? What about me?" Eve's lungs emptied as she flung the question from her heart and left it dangling among the icicles in the trees. Strawberry suddenly skidded, stumbled, and went into a reckless slide.

Ma's angry expression was the last image Eve saw before the horse's abrupt, skidding halt sent her fly-ing. For an instant the world was alive in brilliant, blinding shades of icy-white tree limbs dangling in the wind. The world reaching out to Eve.

All at once everything, even the bright, white snow, turned to blackness.

Scene Two

At first Eve was afraid to move. Her arm hurt. So did her back and legs. Strawberry made a snorting sound and nudged her with her nose.

"OK, OK, I can see that you're fine," Eve said, gently rolling onto her side. Gradually, she tested her body, placing her weight on one foot, then the other. Nothing appeared broken or mangled.

Except her clothes, which were covered with soft, muddy snow.

Eve heaved herself back onto the horse. Strawberry gave another snort. Eve guided the horse back to the trail. She gazed at the late-afternoon sky, noting that Christmas Day was fast turning into Christmas evening and light in the gauzy sky was fading. Fading, Eve thought, like her plans for the future.

When Eve arrived back at the stable, the North Star blazed above the barn. Eve gazed intently at the star before dismounting and leading Strawberry into the stable.

"You look a mess."

Eve jumped, startled. The voice had come out of nowhere.

"Must you always be ridiculous?" Al walked out of the shadows. Eve held on tightly to Strawberry's reins.

Avoiding eye contact with Al, Eve led the horse into the stall, then retrieved the brush.

"She's going to let you do it, you know. Be in the play, I mean. Aunt Mary talked her into it. One catch, though. You still have to work a few hours a week and earn a little money, but, as usual, you'll get what you want." Al sank heavily onto a bale of hay.

Strawberry snorted at Al, who shrank away from the animal. "I hate horses," she said.

"No you don't. You're afraid of horses," Eve said. "There's a difference."

"Well, whatever."

A few minutes passed. Strawberry settled down and shook her mane, appreciating the good brushing.

"Remember when we used to come up here in the summer?" Al said.

Eve stopped brushing. Yes, she did remember.

"Remember? I wrote that story about horses and how they were magic."

Eve nodded, smiling. "Yeah, and I remember we turned your story into a production."

Both girls laughed.

"We used to have a lot of fun," Al mumbled.

"I'm sorry about letting it out, I mean, slipping it out, I mean. . . ." Eve stopped, then started again. "I didn't mean to tell Aunt Mary. I was angry, at Ma, mostly. I guess the good Lord will make a way."

Al rolled her eyes. "So she's back. Good Eve."

"What are you talking about?" Eve could feel Al setting a trap.

"I thought for sure you were finally going to get real and stop acting, but I can see you're back to playing your role. Good Eve. Good girl." Eve felt sliced open and exposed. "Ma was trippin' tonight, as usual, but one thing she said was true for me, too. I can't wait to meet the real Eve." Eve braced herself, but not against the cold. She, too, wondered when she would meet the real Eve.

Al walked away and Eve called out, "By the way, Erick Ross from drama group said to be sure and tell you hello. And good luck. I didn't know you two were so . . . close."

Al glared at Eve before opening the stall door and walking toward the house. Long after her sister had reached the house, Eve brushed Strawberry and wondered once more:

Could Erick Ross be the father of Al's baby?

Act Six

Scene One

Scene One

January came and went, and Eve followed a familiar schedule, balancing play rehearsals with working one day a week after school at her mother's office.

Around the house she wore one silly hat after another as she washed and ironed and stacked and folded loads of laundry. She mopped bathroom floors, carried boxes of old clothes to the church basement for donation, cooked dinner at least twice a week for the family. She did it all without complaining about Ma's nit-picking or lack of praise for her good grades or anything else. All to gain her mother's love, so it would be easier to break away when the summer came.

February storms no doubt drove the groundhog back into its hole. At least, that was the word around town, as folks continued to gossip about the weather.

The winds died to a low grumble as play rehearsal ended. Eve and Bethany trudged along the deserted sidewalk toward home. Without planning it, the girls wound up in a familiar spot—the hilltop behind First Baptist.

"Don't you wish you could fly?" asked Bethany. She sank down to the ground and sat on the tail of her coat.

Eve flopped down beside her, staring at the white sky and smelling the fresh, pine-scented cold. Below, the church parking lot bustled with cars and vans.

"Isaiah has a nasty cough," Bethany said with a sigh.

"Oh no!"

Bethany nodded. "I love him, but we're cooling it this week because of, you know, the germs and all. Just as well, though. I get the feeling he's getting tired of just handholding."

Bethany and Eve flung themselves backward into a heap of soft snow. Eve swept out her arms and legs, slashing out the shape of an angel, and Bethany joined in.

They were being goofy, letting off steam. Exhausted, the two lay panting. Bethany whispered, "Everything is changing so fast."

Eve nodded.

"What's up with you and Al? She still mad?"

Eve shrugged, then propped herself on her elbows. "She ignores me, mostly." Bethany was the only person with whom she had dared to share Al's secret. Five months. That was how far along Al was. Although she'd begun wearing loose-fitting clothes, few people could really tell.

"Hey, Eve, do you ever think about what it's going to be like to be an aunt?" Bethany gave Eve a nudge.

"I try not to think about it because I don't want to make a mistake and accidentally *talk* about it. You know, we're not allowed to discuss anything real in our house."

"Do you think Al was in love? With the guy, I mean?"

Eve shook her head. "Doesn't seem like it. Who knows?"

A moment passed and Eve turned her face toward Bethany. "You said before that you love Isaiah. Do you think you love him enough to, you know?"

Bethany rolled onto her back and stared at the thin blanket of sky between her and heaven. "I do love him, and sometimes I think I'm ready. Other times I know I'm definitely not ready. Not really 'not ready,' but just don't want to, you know, be doing that yet. "If you had the chance to be with you-know-who, would you?" Bethany flashed a shy grin.

Eve sighed. "I feel like a fiend most of the time, B. I can't stop thinking about him."

"But do you think about him because you really love him? Or is it, you know, just physical? Just about doing it? Love and sex, they're so not the same thing."

Eve swallowed a lump in her throat that felt like a snowball. Love and sex, they were, indeed, so not the same. Still, she felt a prickle of annoyance at Bethany's question. Of course she wouldn't consider doing it just to be physical. She wasn't going to do it with just anybody.

Lucious wasn't just anybody. But did she really love him? She sure thought about him all the time. Thought about him in ways that she never thought about any other boy. Thought about . . . *it*.

But love?

Eve threw open her arms and shouted to the sky: "Lord! Give me a sign!"

She and Bethany rocked against one another, giggling and holding on to one another for support, until, at the same time they spotted a pair of heavy boots.

Have mercy! The Lord hadn't sent just a sign, why, he'd sent a walking billboard.

Lucious had snuck up on the girls. He held a huge sketch pad beneath his arm, and a camera was strapped around his neck. Eve had to blink twice to make sure she saw what she thought she did. The reflection of late-afternoon sun off the snow created a halo around him.

"Angels in the snow, huh?" Lucious said, nodding toward the imprints.

"I was, we—we were on our way home," Eve said. What did that mean? *We were on our way home. . . .* Her words got tangled. She felt stupid.

Lucious sank to his knees and Eve rose to hers. They were at eye level, his gaze confident, hers unsteady. "You live in the woods behind the church?" His voice was smiling and so were his full lips.

"Hi, Lucious," Bethany called out. "What are you doing up here?"

"Hey, Lil B. What's up?" he said to Bethany. Her older sister, Mariah Bertina, called Bertie for short, was Big B.

Lucious opened his sketch pad, and Eve noticed his hands. Dark smudges coated his fingers as he grasped a thin, charcoal stick. He gazed intently at the church below. After several quick strokes he broke into a wide grin. "I like going up into the hills and taking wildlife pictures. I also like sketching the kids playing down in the churchyard from up here. They can't see me and won't get to posing and whatnot."

He looked at Eve.

"You should let me sketch you sometime. How many more times you gonna make me ask?"

"Man, you're really good," Bethany said.

Lucious smiled broadly. "I hope so. I'm working on my portfolio."

"You're going to be a model?" Bethany said.

"A model?"

"Well, I mean, after the posters . . ." Bethany's hand flew to cover her mouth.

"What pos . . ." Lucious began, then he shook his head and laughed. "Oh, you mean, *The Posters*. Did you see 'em? The posters of me?"

Eve bit her lip and shook her head vigorously, "No. No I didn't."

She was lying, and she read in his expression that he knew she was lying. Lucious turned toward Bethany, who was nodding. "I saw one. You were so . . ." she stopped as her eyes connected with Eve's. Bethany's blushing cheeks flamed as bright as her red hair.

"Naked?" Lucious finished Bethany's sentence. His laughter was soft and low in his throat. "No, I'm not the model type. A friend at the community college needed someone to pose for a life-drawing class she was taking. Who knew she'd get all wacko and use the Polaroids she took to make all those posters? You never really know what people are up to, now, do you?"

Eve, who had knelt beside Lucious, drew in a sharp breath, rocked backward, and sat on her butt. Lucious clung tightly to the sketch pad and made no move to pull Eve upright. "The portfolio I'm working on now is for art school."

Eve started brushing snow and wet grass off her backside. Lucious winked at her and said, "Don't worry. When I sketch you, I promise, no Polaroids, no scandal." Then he brushed his finger along the line of her jaw, letting it drop to the gold heart floating on the chain around her neck. His fingers lingered for a moment, then dropped away.

Eve's heart skipped a beat as she wondered what it would be like to pose for Lucious Prior.

Scene Three

Onstage, Abigail Williams and her young, Puritan play-mates were having a rendezvous in the woods, dancing provocatively. The scene with Abigail and her friends was highly charged, one that set the tone for the story—young women forced to repress themselves unleashing their inhibitions in the dark, secret forest.

"Stop! Stop! Stop!" cried Joel.

Joel rubbed his forehead, his eyes closed. "Ladies, you are supposed to be puritanical women who, in a moment of frenzy, allow yourselves to dance freely in the cover of the deep woods. Not drunken spring-breakers shaking your booties for a Girls Gone Wild video!"

Joel—lovely, delicate Joel—shuddered when he said *booties*. Laughter erupted from the rear of the auditorium where Glow Worm was working with the other Puritans.

Joel shook his head. "I'm sorry; I'm sorry. I didn't

mean to snap. I'm sure you guys in the rear, based on what I've been seeing this week, are having problems of your own." He cocked his eyebrow until the snickering stopped.

Eve removed her derby hat and ran her fingers through her hair. As Abigail she was leading the girls. Did that make her head Girl Gone Wild? Rehearsals had grown intense. The first few weeks, they had just been running lines, practicing dialogue, seeing how different actors looked onstage with other actors. Now rehearsals required focus and concentration.

"Everybody, let's gather round and chat a bit, shall we?" Joel said.

All the actors came down to the front of the auditorium and found seats. Eve sat on the edge of the stage; Bethany hopped up beside her.

"How many of you have your copies of the play?" Joel asked. Several hands shot up, some waving *The Crucible*.

"See, that's our first point of discussion. A play is a production, not something you can wave in the air. What you-all are reading is the text. There is a difference. We're trying to put on a production. Now, who here understands what an allegory is?"

Eve tucked her legs Indian style beneath her. For the next thirty minutes, Joel explained how Arthur Miller, author of *The Crucible*, was fed up with McCarthyism.

When he asked who knew what McCarthyism was, Jeremy Early—the boy playing Deputy Governor Danforth—raised his hand and said, "Someone who hates people named McCarthy."

"No, Jeremy, that is incorrect. McCarthyism was named after Senator Joseph McCarthy, famous in the fifties for using the United States Congress to investigate communism. A lot of actors and artists in this country were victimized by that ungodly witch hunt," Joel said, clasping his throat self-consciously.

"To protest against writers and actors and others being falsely labeled communists, Arthur Miller researched another phenomenon in history when people suffered for being falsely accused: the Salem witch trials. An allegory," Joel explained, "is when you take one event to represent another symbolically."

Bethany leaned over and whispered, "Arthur Miller could have had enough for two plays if he'd used my mom and her false allegations as inspiration!"

Eve stifled a giggle. She lay flat, her belly pressed against the stage floor. She thought about Joel's message and she thought about herself. His explanation made sense.

Had Abigail started off trying to be good but given in to her *other* side?

Eve raised her hand and asked, "Did Abigail really believe in the beginning that her friend Betty was possessed by a demon?"

Joel shook his head. "No."

"She was just a troublemaking little tramp!" said a girl from the back. Color and heat rushed to Eve's cheeks.

"I don't see her that way!" Eve took a deep breath and told herself to stay calm.

"Good, Eve, good," said Joel. "How would you describe Abigail?"

Eve played with the brim of her hat. "Abigail knows what she wants. She's determined," Eve said.

"Yes, Eve. Yes! And what is it that Abigail wants?"

"Another woman's man, Mr. Cryer, and that's why if this was modern times, she'd definitely be starring in one of them Girls Gone Wild videos!" said a girl from the second row. More laughter.

"Call me Joel, people, not Mr. Cryer." He returned his attention to the stage.

"Eve?"

"Yes, Joel. Um . . ."

"What does Abigail want?" Joel said.

"She wants John Proctor."

Joel nodded. "And what else?"

Eve thought for a moment. "Alive. She wants to be

alive. In that small town with small-minded people, she's a girl without a lot of—um, what's the right word—choices."

"So that gave her the right to be messing 'round with somebody's husband?" said the heckler from the second row.

Eve ignored her. "I think maybe she got tired of waiting for the life that everyone expected her to have; she decided to go for what she wanted for herself. And what she wanted was John Proctor."

"Very good, Eve! Very, very good!" Joel climbed the stairs from stage left. "All right, people, let's knock off for the day. You're getting there, all of you, but it's time now to really think about the emotional depths of your characters."

Joel placed his hand on Eve's shoulder. "I think it's wonderful that you're beginning to dig deeper to discover the real Abigail. She is a complex, intriguing character." The *real* Abigail. Eve wondered if she'd ever dig deep enough to uncover the *real* Eve.

Eve walked toward the heavy drapes when suddenly a hand reached out.

"Oh!" Eve cried.

Air rushed from her lungs, her knees went soft, and Eve found herself tumbling to the floor.

"Eve!" Lucious whispered against her ear, picking

her up. She wasn't unconscious, just too embarrassed to look in his face. He held her just above the floor.

"Oh my! Is she all right?" Joel rushed over. Eve scrambled to stand upright. Lucious smelled warm and vaguely like fresh apples. Eve felt a tingly sensation that started in her chest and spread all over her. She exhaled. She wondered if he'd been stocking fruit at the grocery. She wondered if his suddenly appearing, just as he had on the hill above the church, was another sign.

"I'm fine, I'm fine," Eve said, giving perhaps her best performance of the afternoon. "I just took a tumble; that's all."

"Well, for heaven's sake, be more careful! You're our star, dear," Joel said, then turned to Lucious. "So, are you here to talk about art direction?"

"Sure, man, give me a sec," Lucious said. He turned back to Eve, reached into his pocket, and pulled out an apple. Bright red with a stem. "Take it," he said. "It'll keep the doctor away."

"Thanks." Eve felt the weight of the apple in her hand, felt her hand tremble. "I blew off lunch today. Guess I got a little dizzy."

Lucious stepped closer, and Eve could hear her own breathing.

"You need to take better care of yourself."

She nodded. The two faced each other, silent. Eve

counted her heartbeats till Lucious said, "Hey, I heard what you said about that character, Abigail, wanting to be alive and not wanting to be what everybody expected. You know a lot for a good girl, don't you?"

His voice had dipped into a husky whisper, and Eve couldn't help thinking how, when he said it, *good girl* didn't sound quite so good.

"I gotta go," she said. She turned and walked quickly off the stage. In her mind she could already taste the sweetness of the apple.

Scene Four

Scene Four

Several days passed before Eve saw Lucious again. February's swirling grayness began to lessen, but March still managed to get icy now and again. As Eve passed the Golden Apple Grocery on her way home from rehearsal, Lucious appeared on the sidewalk ahead.

He was coming toward her so fast that he bumped into her.

"Lucious?" Eve's voice was tentative. When he turned, heat from his gaze singed her. She took a step back.

"Sorry," he barked. Then repeated "sorry" in a softer tone.

"You all right?" she asked.

"I'm just sick of working around all these lame busters all day. Always busting my chops, busting my hump about how somebody like me is never going to make it as an artist. How the type of person I am never makes it past Eden city limits. They think they know who I am, but they don't. For real, I'm not spending the rest of my life jammed up in Eden. I won't let that happen." He moved swiftly down the sidewalk as Eve struggled to match his stride. He stopped abruptly, his brow drawing deep question marks.

"You down with me?"

Eve didn't understand his question, but didn't want to say no, so she nodded. He took her hand in his, held it tight, and said, "C'mon."

They walked briefly for two more blocks, Eve jogging across slick patches of ice to keep up. Lucious muttered to himself, and, although he gripped her hand, he acted as though he were alone.

In the middle of a run-down block, he pointed to a window. "I live up there. C'mon." No sooner had Eve glimpsed the tiny window, than Lucious yanked her in its direction and pulled her through a door and up the stairs.

Lucious lived in a small apartment above a music store. The bedroom and living room were one and the same. The kitchenette revealed a tiny area that included a hot plate. Rows and rows of drawings and paintings, some in colorful pastels, others in shadowy charcoal, still others in thick oils, covered the walls all the way around.

"Did you do all these?" Eve reddened. Stupid question.

Lucious tossed her a sideways glance as he flung his insulated gloves against the sofa. "I just need to draw and clear my head," he said, ignoring her transparent question. "Back in a sec."

He disappeared behind the bathroom door, and Eve exhaled for the first time since she'd bumped into him. If her mother ever found out she was up here . . . .

Eve's gaze went from image to image on Lucious's walls. Portraits. Landscapes. Blue-ink waterfalls. Pastels of the gnarled, withered features of old people.

"I know I have talent," Lucious said, coming out of the bathroom.

Eve was so entranced with the intricate details of his work, his voice seemed far away. When he cleared his throat, she felt herself travel backward, out of the blue-ink hills bordered by a blue-ink lake. Breathlessly she said, "Your work is amazing!"

He looked at her as though seeing her for the first time. He asked, "You think so?" He sounded hesitant and insecure.

"Lucious! Look at what you've done. Look at all this." Eve pointed from the pencil landscapes, clearly drawn at Bella Creek, to the pastel charcoal of an older woman with a kind face. Eve had seen her at church. His grandmother.

"I have to do something," Lucious said. "I need you with me. Are you in?"

"Well . . ." Eve hesitated. What was he thinking? His eyes had gone from angry to bright. Almost smiling. But she was supposed to be on a bus headed to her mom's office.

"Don't say no, Eve. Please?"

Eve trembled. Lucious Prior needed her.

"See, the thing is, I have to meet my mom." She tried to sound casual.

He whipped out his cell phone and handed it to her. "Cancel. Please? For me?"

Eve listened to the electronic beeps, her heart racing faster with each tone.

Then she punched in the number.

"Attorney Sid Stein's office, may I help you?" Mrs. Noble said, in her usual, professional voice.

"Hi, Ma!" Eve said brightly.

Immediately Ruth Ann Noble's voice changed. "Where are you? You're supposed to be on the bus coming here."

"I know, Ma, but practice is running late. I really don't think I can make it today."

"We had a deal, Eve. . . ."

"Yes, Ma, but rehearsals are starting to get longer; that's all."

Silence at the other end. Eve looked at Lucious with crossed fingers.

"All right, Eve. But you'd better be where you say you are, hear me? And you'd better not let your chores at home slide, either."

"Yes, Ma." The lie came easy. Eve clicked off and returned the phone to Lucious.

Eve had never told such a lie to her mother. Yet somehow, standing in Lucious's apartment, doing the forbidden and unthinkable seemed normal, exhilarating.

Lucious said he needed to draw, and he did his best work up at his grandmother's cabin. Later Eve would think back and not be able to remember putting on her gloves and following Lucious outside and down the block to his truck. The two remained silent for the first few miles. Eve bumped her head against the glass of the passenger window as they drove into the country. Landscapes raced past the windows matching the zip-zip pace of Eve's emotions.

Have I gone insane?

"It means a lot you did this for me, trusting me like this. Sometimes . . ."

Eve's head snapped up. Lucious smacked the steering wheel.

"Sometimes you get a reputation. Sometimes you do stupid things, make mistakes. I was probably twelve when I had my first drink. After my old man took off, I bet I drank a hell of a lot more than . . . well, whatever. People say things about me, think I'm no good, but I don't swing that way no more. My art means everything to me, everything. I'd never mess that up."

Lucious put on the blinker for exit 33b and headed down a two-lane road that Eve recognized. It was the same road that led to Aunt Mary's farm. She felt her muscles tense up in her neck and tried to remain calm.

"Did your old man ever work for P-Johns downtown?" Lucious glanced over at Eve, and she nodded. Preston-Johns Automotive Factory's abandoned warehouses lined the town like haunted houses.

"He drives a truck now, right? Your old man?"

"Daddy's been driving a truck for years," Eve said.

"You're lucky. When the shop closed down, my old man split. Left my mom, his mom, his kids. A few years later, my mom died of cancer. My younger brother and sister went to live with relatives in Georgia but everybody thought, with my grandparents getting older, maybe I should stay here, help 'em out and all."

At first his words had raced like a locomotive. Now they were losing steam. He exhaled, his breath fogging the windshield. The truck sputtered along and creaked on its hinges as he came to a stop sign.

"That thing last spring, you know, with the posters . . ."

he was almost whispering.

Eve sat rock still, afraid to look at him, afraid to move. For fifteen minutes she'd listened to him rant and spew. Never had she seen anyone, except maybe her mother, release such glorious, beautiful, raw anger. *He must be the bravest boy in the world*, she thought.

"My grandfather did the best he could, raising me, teaching me to fish, and stuff like that. Him and Granny encouraged me to stay in school, encouraged me to draw. Man," Lucious released a harsh laugh, "he really loved to see me with that sketch pad. He wanted to see me graduate more than anything. All he wanted was to see me graduate. He died last March, just about a year ago."

He pressed down on the accelerator.

"They think they hurt me by keeping me out of that stupid graduation ceremony because of some damn, naked pictures on posters that weren't even my fault. Like I cared." His words sped up again, radiating heat.

"What the hell did I care? My grandfather wasn't going to be there. My mom or my old man couldn't be there. Granny was too sick last spring, mostly from a broken heart. Think I cared about some stupid gradua-tion? Huh? Why should I care?"

The heater didn't work and below-freezing air filled the space between them. Eve wanted to look away, shield herself from the directness of his gaze, but she couldn't.

With trembling fingers, carefully, so carefully, Eve reached across the foam rubber tearing through the seat and touched his hand.

He pulled away, and Eve clenched her fingers into a fist. She picked up a couple of CD cases. Gospel CDs.

"Your grandmother's?" she asked, thinking of the gentle, old woman now living at the retirement home where Eve sometimes volunteered.

"Mine."

Eve's eyes widened. Lucious's laugh was dry and mirthless. "Oh, so you're just like the rest of 'em, huh? Can't imagine shiftless, troublemaking Lucious kicking back in his truck listening to gospel?"

Eve shook her head. "No!" she cried.

"Maybe this was a mistake. I should have known you wouldn't be different from any of the rest!"

Eve felt like she'd been sucker punched. "That's not true."

She felt foolish. Had she ruined things with Lucious before they'd even started?

Lucious sat forward, slamming his palm against the steering wheel. Then he was silent, and the silence drove Eve crazy.

"I'm sorry, Eve, really," he said. "I'm just . . . just . . ."

"Fed up?" asked Eve.

He nodded. "Yeah, fed up." After a second, he gave her a half smile. "But I know how to make it better, if you're willing to help."

And that was how it started, the sneaking away, the sketches, the lies. Each time they visited the cabin, Lucious would slip into a near trance, posing Eve on the sofa or somewhere outside, making one sketch after another after another, until his fingers would cramp and bleed charcoal.

They almost never talked, not while he was working. She'd catch glimpses of the sketches and feel awe at the intensity he captured in her eyes or the exact way he re-created her body. No matter what she was feeling, Lucious found a way to highlight it in his sketches.

And he did a good job of getting her back downtown around 5:30 P.M., just in time to run home before her mom and Al. At times the desire to share her adventures with her sister burned within her. How she missed having Al to talk to.

Scene Five

Scene Five

"How far along is she now? Your sister?" Lucious kept his eyes on the road. He and Eve were heading to the cabin. Eve had never discussed Al and was surprised he knew her twin was pregnant.

"What?"

"Your sister. I saw her the other day," he said carefully. "She's sticking out pretty good. I didn't know she had a man."

"I didn't know you knew my sister," Eve said.

"She's your twin, and she's pregnant. You're the one who wears the hats," he joked, flicking the bill of her old-fashioned, knit cap. "She wore baseball hats, too, or something like that this summer. At the park, right? The two of you worked there?"

Eve's heart started speeding. She had dreaded discussing Al with Lucious. Why? Was she afraid of what she might find out? "You met my sister?"

"Never said I met her."

"Have you?" She kept her eyes straight ahead.

"I get around. I know a lot of people." He didn't speak for several seconds, but when he did he abruptly changed the subject. "You and me, today should be our last day."

The truck lurched to a halt under the dense trees that encircled the tiny cabin. In the weeks since she'd started accompanying Lucious, Eve had felt herself change. So much of what she'd spent her lifetime pushing deep down—her feelings, her fears, her wishes—had risen closer and closer to the surface. Lucious took away the dull emptiness. Yet at times she felt close to falling over the edge and into a world she couldn't imagine.

At rehearsals Joel had noticed the change and praised her. "Your delivery is so commanding, Eve. You have so much more confidence," he said.

Did that come from lying? Betraying her mother's trust?

Did it come from all the roles she played off stage in the only show that truly mattered?

Lucious had never so much as kissed her. He hadn't laid a hand on her. Yet everything about their little sneak-away trips felt romantic and forbidden. She'd grown to love the talks they had in the truck. They talked about everything, personal talk that Eve wouldn't share with anyone else.

"You didn't answer me!" Eve's voice rose. The look in Lucious's eyes told her she'd caught him off guard.

sherri winston

"What?"

"You heard me. How do you know my sister?"

Lucious's eyes narrowed as if he was about to say something, then thought better of it. He sighed, "Your sister, Al, she doesn't like me very much."

"So you know her?"

"Yeah. I know her. She thinks I'm a delinquent. C'mon, let's roll."

And roll they did. Rolled the truck to a stop.

Inside the cabin Eve heard her teeth chatter from the damp chill. Lucious went to the fireplace and lit some logs. Within minutes warmth flooded the tiny room. Eve pulled off her coat and bulky snowflake sweater, keeping on her T-shirt. Lucious stood behind her, his nearness causing more heat than the fire.

Eve turned suddenly and found herself in his arms. His tongue slid easily into her mouth. They were Nia Long and Larenz Tate in *love jones*. The heat made Eve crazy. Her brain tried to dial up Grandma Peaches and one of her million arguments against sins of the flesh, but the memory was fuzzy.

His touch was strong and confident. A few weeks before, Eve and Bethany had ditched class to catch a chick-flick-classic matinee, *How Stella Got Her Groove Back*. Eve had wondered if she would ever have a groove, let alone get it back.

142

"No, wait . . . no," Eve stammered. Penetrating the numbness that so often kept her from feeling anything, Lucious's touch made her feel everything everywhere. She felt herself being led. He was walking forward; she was walking backward. The backs of her legs bumped something. The sofa. As quickly as she recognized where she was, she found herself tilting, off-balance, falling over the edge . . .

Lucious was on top of her before she could move.

Then the scene changed. She could hear it in her breathing. Need. The heels of her hands, which seconds earlier had been curved to help push Lucious away, now worked with her fingers.

Pulling.

She opened her mouth and found his tongue touching hers, her fingers clutching his shirt. She could feel him, Lucious, the weight of him, the solidness of his body.

Eve tried to picture Daphne Rose from her romance novel, tried to picture Drew Barrymore as an empowered Cinderella, tried to conjure images from her favorite romances.

Blank.

Too much heat.

"Wait . . . no, wait . . ."

Not Eve. Lucious, wanting to slow down.

"You want to stop?" she panted.

"I've just been messing around with you, you know, having fun. Let's not take it too far," he said. Right then, a ringing sound startled Eve. It was coming from inside Lucious's pants.

She knew alarms had been ringing in her head, but his alarm was in his pants pockets.

"Hello?" His voice was heavy as he spoke into the cell phone. He rolled off the sofa and left Eve to catch her breath. He murmured into the phone far enough away so she couldn't hear. Then, as if nothing had happened, he returned and said, "C'mon, let's finish the sketches."

Eve sat in a straight-back chair. Now she knew how shame and humiliation felt. He hadn't mentioned anything about what had just happened. He'd pushed her away, then gone about his business.

When Lucious finished sketching, he asked Eve to sit still. He produced a tiny sketchbook. After several furious pen strokes, he said, "For you."

Eve stared, and a miniature image stared back at her. "How do you get so much detail in such a small space? And so quickly?"

Lucious grinned. "Like it?"

She didn't know if she'd been feeling anger or guilt or shame or what, but whatever it was started breaking away, and Eve felt lighter, freer. "It's wonderful! Thank you!" When she reached out to hug him, he pulled her into his arms.

"I like you, Eve Noble. You know that, right?"

She nodded.

"I like hanging with you and messing with you, and if my life wasn't so crazy right now, I'd be all over you. But this is not a good time for us right now. We're still cool, right?"

Again she nodded.

Lucious sighed. "We have to get going."

In the truck Eve's lips tingled from the force of Lucious's earlier kisses. She tugged her lip between her teeth, stealing a glance at him.

Before she had spent time with him, thinking about him had made her all tingly and uncertain, silly and excited. Sitting beside him, remembering his touch, remembering his eyes locked with hers, made the feelings more intense.

And more confusing. As much as she didn't want to, she thought about the perfectly round, basketball belly mushrooming beneath Al's clothes. She couldn't imagine Al being as confused as she felt right now. Eve sank back against the seat and looked up to see Lucious staring over at her.

His dark eyes were warm and soft. Eve looked away

and felt a tremble race from her chest into her belly. She had always imagined that having him look at her like that would be the greatest, happiest thing in the world. Instead, it just confused her more.

Scene Six

For two weeks Bad Eve remained silent about her growing lusts and sinful wants. She'd sit in church and try to
listen, although she couldn't concentrate much. Lucious
worked on sets several times a week. He'd ask Eve to
help him, and she'd jumped at the chance.

At first the nearness of Lucious Prior made Eve dizzy.
The same way Miss Drew Barrymore must have felt in
Never Been Kissed.

Even though there was no lip tasting going on, Eve
felt the thrill of Lucious over and over. And in today's
rehearsal Eve was thinking about Lucious and trembling a little. She wasn't concentrating on the scene.

"Stop!" Joel Cryer called out from the wings. Eve was
facing Erick Ross.

"Tell me, Eve. What are you visualizing right now as
you do this scene?"

No way was she going to tell Joel what was on her
mind. Same thing as always lately—Lucious.

She took a deep breath. It was the scene in which John Proctor comes to confront Abigail about the rampant claims of witchcraft she and her friends had been making. Abigail pleads with John to return the love they once shared. He rebuffs her.

"I'm thinking about . . ." Lucious's hammer hung in midair. Everyone, it seemed, was waiting.

"Remember the movie *Dirty Dancing*? There's a scene when Baby, the main character, is trying to convince the guy she loves . . . I can't remember the character's name, but Patrick Swayze played the role. Anyway, Baby is trying to convince him that she isn't like the other snobby people at the country club. I was thinking about how much she wanted him to see her for who she really was. I thought maybe that's what Abigail was trying, too. She wants John Proctor to see her as she is, not as some hysterical troublemaker."

Eve felt proud of her answer, and Joel nodded and praised her. "Good, Eve, good. You're on the right track. But concentrate more on drawing those feelings out of yourself, not from movies you've seen." Eve nodded, but her mind went back to Lucious. She wondered if she would ever feel comfortable using her feelings for Lucious to flesh out a character in a play. Days passed and Eve continued to rehearse and help Lucious with set building.

Alone in the south hall, painting scenery, Eve and Lucious talked, and when they did, Eve's mind read their dialogue as though it were a script:

> *Lucious: Johnny Castle.*
>
> *Eve: Huh?*
>
> *Lucious: Remember a few days ago when you were rehearsing and started talking about that movie?*
>
> *Eve: Dirty Dancing?*
>
> *Lucious: Yeah. Anyway, the guy's name in that movie was Johnny Castle.*

Later that same day, still painting, the dialogue continued:

> *Lucious: A brother is beat. I've started a part-time job working a few nights a week at the music store downstairs.*
>
> *Eve: Why are you working two jobs?*
>
> *Lucious (eyebrows raised): A brother gots responsibilities. You know?*

The dialogue continued late at night. Lucious had given Eve a disposable cell phone. Said he had it lying around. Said she could use it when they talked at night so she wouldn't disturb her family. She had asked once why he had so many phones. He'd told her he had "a hook-up." Whatever.

Lucious: So, you ready to be an auntie?

Eve: Hadn't thought about it.

Lucious: Is Al ready to be a mom?

Eve: She's not keeping the baby. She's putting it, um, I mean, him or her, up for adoption. So I guess she's not ready to be a mom.

Lucious: She's very smart, your sister. But putting her baby up for adoption, that's a big step. I hope she knows what she's doing.

Eve: My sister always knows what she's doing.

Lucious: If that was true, maybe she wouldn't be pregnant.

Then came the scene with Lucious that would stick in her head long after she left with her family to visit Aunt Mary at the farm:

Lucious: That baby's not mine.

Eve: Huh? Lucious? Lucious, what did you say?

Lucious: That rumor last year, about the Mayes girl. That was bogus. Me and Tracey Mayes went out a few times, and she was a nice girl. We didn't do anything. But people tried to make out like I was the father of her baby. It wasn't true.

Eve: Why are you telling me this?

Lucious: I want you to know I don't have a baby out there somewhere, unclaimed. I wouldn't do that. Just wanted you to know.

Act Seven

Scene One

Eve lay staring at the rough-hewn ceiling in Aunt Mary's second-floor guest room. Light seeped in from the hall. The house was quiet now. On Daddy and Ma's twenty-fifth wedding anniversary, Aunt Mary had surprised them with dinner and a get-away trip to Florida. They had left the next day, and now the twins were sharing the large room at the far end of the hall, just like when they were kids. Neither girl had said much to the other since the last time they had been at Aunt Mary's. A mumbled hello, a grunted phone message. Not much else though Eve prayed and pictured many vivid scenes in which Al would need her and reach out for her and she, Eve, would be there ready and willing.

"Can you believe how happy Ma looked last night?" asked Eve, her voice hesitating. Al was lying on the opposite bed, her back to Eve and her knees tucked toward her chest.

A grunt. Eve hadn't really expected much else. But

when Al spoke, her voice soft and gruff at the same time, it startled Eve.

"What I can't believe is that Ma and Daddy are warming their toes in the sand while we're up here freezing our butts off," Al grumbled.

The sheets rustled as both girls jostled for comfort in the twin beds.

"Hard to get comfortable with this stupid belly in the way," said Al. She seemed to have sprouted an enormous belly overnight.

"Al . . ." Eve faltered, then decided, what the hell. "Al, remember a few months back, when we were in your room? Was it really like that? I mean, did he hurt you? Did he . . . force you?"

In Eve's mind she'd carried a horrific image of Al, serious and shy Al, bookworm Al, being lured into the darkness and forced to submit to all sorts of disgusting acts, which led to her pregnancy.

"I need another pillow," Al said bluntly.

Eve paused. Al cast her a sideways glance. "A pillow? Can you get me one?"

Eve sighed and went to the trunk at the foot of Al's bed. She pulled one out.

Al shoved the pillow behind her back without a "thank you," not that Eve had really expected one. Eve climbed back into bed and was about to go to sleep when her sister's voice again caught her by surprise.

"No," Al said softly.

Eve turned back and frowned.

"No? No what?"

"No, I wasn't raped or brutalized or taken advantage of or whatever. You want to know what really happened? I messed up. I'm being punished because I messed up. Period."

"So you weren't hurt or anything?"

Al shook her head. "No, it wasn't like that. It . . . it shouldn't have happened. I guess when it comes down to it, I thought he was another kind of person, and he definitely thought I was somebody else." Her tone went flat and hard.

"You really want to put your baby up for adoption?" Eve said.

"You know how hard it was to tell Ma about this," Al hissed. "Can you imagine how she'd have acted if I'd said I wanted to keep it?"

Eve untangled herself from the crisp sheets and rushed to sit beside Al. She grabbed her sister's hand. "Do you want to keep it?"

"No!" Al snatched her hand away.

Eve sat, silent.

"Sorry," said Al.

They both sighed, then Eve asked, "Hey, remember

that time we spent spring break up here and you had that ugly doll with the bald spot? What did you call her?"

"Evil Peach!" Al said, laughing.

"After our bitter, old grandmother. Do it, Al. Do the voice."

Al gave a sly snort, then launched into a brittle-toned recitation of some of Grandma Peaches' favorite sayings:

The whole world is full of sin!
Music videos are for sex maniacs.
Modern women are causing the ruination of the
world.
Being boy crazy will send you straight to hell!

They were still laughing when Eve said, "If she'd been anymore hateful, she could have made the Devil jealous."

Al giggled, and Eve began, "Ma . . ."

". . . hasn't been the same," Al continued.

". . . since Grandma Peaches died," Eve finished. They both looked at each other. How long had it been since one finished the other's thought?

It was after Grandma Peaches' death that Ma stepped in to steer Al's future. Steer her away from Eve—at least that was how Eve felt.

Eve returned to her bed.

"I'm not ready to be a mom," Al said, rolling onto her side. "You and I have been talking forever about escaping Eden."

"Except . . ." Eve began hesitantly, "except we were trying to escape together. Now . . . now you're leaving me."

Al's laugh was bitter. "Well, I'll need a head start if I'm going to make all of Ma's dreams come true."

Both girls turned to face one another.

"Ma looked so happy last night when Aunt Mary surprised her and Daddy with their little, second-honeymoon trip," Eve said.

"I wish I could get away, too. Get far, far away," said Al.

Eve took a chance. "Would you run away with your baby's father?"

Al sort of laughed, but it wasn't quite convincing. "He and I don't have any honeymoons in our future. He was an experiment. I thought I could never fall for him, but the whole thing went too far. I thought he wanted me, and it made me feel . . ." her voice cracked. "Stupid. I was playing a stupid game. I lost."

"Al? I wish he had been your fantasy. I wish he had been a fantasy come true."

Big yawn from Al. "Um, speaking of fantasies, is Lucious Prior still your fantasy?"

Since that day at the cabin, Eve and Lucious had had

limited physical contact. No kissing. A little hugging. But that was it.

Yet, lying on her back in this room with her pregnant sister, Eve understood something she hadn't until now: Eve felt closer to Lucious than she ever had. When he had been her fantasy, he had been made out of wishes and imaginary dialogue, false bravado and manly poses. A handsome, romantic lead, a hero in tight jeans.

Now he was so much more than a fantasy. He was determination and talent, soft caresses and whispers, gospel music and pure desire. He wasn't just a boy, he was . . . a person.

"No," Eve said.

Eve could hear Al turning over in the other bed. "Eve, do you swear there's, um, you know, that you and Lucious are not . . ."

"NO!" The shout burst out. Eve quickly added, lowering her voice, "I mean, no, nothing. I admit it, I've had a thing for him and all. He was my fantasy, but now, now it's different. Now he's more than a fantasy. He's . . . he's a real, real person."

"Careful, Eve. Real can be more dangerous than fantasies."

Eve drifted off with another fantasy—the fantasy of God answering her prayers and Al forgiving her. Would this be the first step toward getting her sister back?

Scene Two

Eve was on the back porch ironing. She hadn't ironed on the porch since that day in November when Al had come home with her news and changed everybody's life.

Eve propped her copy of *The Crucible* just so, and when she began ironing, she studied the lines. In Act One Abigail tries to seduce John Proctor. She thought about Joel's explanation. Thought about the pinned-up, sexual, puritanical fervor.

These girls maybe were feeling things about their bodies, their lives, that they didn't understand, and therefore the only explanation was that they were being marked by the devil.

Eve folded the bright pillowcase and grabbed another from the basket. Abigail and John Proctor had been intimate, Eve knew, when Abigail worked for John Proctor's wife, Elizabeth. ". . . *John—I am waiting for you every night.*" Eve read the line aloud once—then again. She brought the hot iron to a halt and repeated the line. Then she read John Proctor's line: "*I never gave you hope to wait for me.*"

As she folded the next warm pillowcase and bent to place it on the pile, she realized her mother was standing behind her. "Good afternoon, Goody Noble," Eve said, dipping into a slight curtsy.

Ma said, "Eve, we need to talk."

In the living room, Ma stood twisting her hands. Then she sat down across from Eve, her fingers rubbing the conservative, blue skirt of her conservative, blue suit. She crossed her feet at the ankles.

"We're going to see Dr. Bernard," Ma said. When Eve frowned, Ma continued, "He's . . . he's my gynecologist."

Eve sat back, dumbfounded. She quickly raised her hand to cover her mouth. "Oh Ma! Are you . . . I mean, you're not..."

Was Ma pregnant, too? Had the whole world gone nuts?

Ma snapped, "Of course not. We're not going for me, Eve; we're going for you."

It took almost a full minute for the meaning to seep into Eve's brain. *We're going for me. For me?*

Then she remembered Bethany and the conclusions her mother had jumped to. How Bethany's mom had assumed that because Bethany had a boyfriend, she must be having sex.

"Ma! No! Why?"

"Because your sister has told me how you're still intent on sniffing around that hooligan boy, that Lucious Prior. No matter what anyone says to you, you seem determined to . . ."

Eve felt a single tear on her cheek. Her mother's tone softened, and she shook her head. "Eve, we have an appointment. We should go."

Eve was dumbstruck. After all the antisex preaching, hearing Ma talk about birth control sounded like science fiction. Ruth Ann pulled on her coat and gloves; Eve didn't move. Her mother repeated, "Eve, time to go."

"I'm not making the same mistake with you," Ma said, as Eve sat staring out the car window. "God knows that if Al wasn't smart enough to stay out of trouble, I can't expect more from you." Eve shivered when she thought how much her mother sounded like Grandma Peaches.

When the exam was over, Eve sat in stony silence while her mother drove up to a pharmacy window to fill a prescription for birth control pills.

"I did it for your own good," Ma said. "Stop your pouting. And keep your mouth shut about this. Your father doesn't have to know everything that goes on."

Eve looked straight ahead. She was thinking about Al. The sisters had spent a week together while their parents vacationed in Florida. They hadn't exactly been pals, but Eve thought they had made some progress.

Until now. Al had told Ma about Lucious. How could she? Maybe this was Al's way of getting even.

Eve tried to get into character. Tried to prepare herself for the confrontation that would occur between her and Al.

Think good thoughts. Think good girl. Think Doris Day or Julia Roberts or whole milk or kittens.

But when she walked into the house and saw Al on the sofa, thoughts of wholesome kittens and pink-cheeked Doris Day flew out the door.

"You are hateful, Alexandra. A rotten, hateful witch!"

"Stop being so melodramatic. I didn't do anything to you!" Al spat.

"You betrayed me! I thought . . . well . . ."

"What you told me was a bunch of nonsense about Lucious and how much you want to be with him, like this family doesn't have enough problems right now?"

Eve took a momentary step back. The nerve! "There's nothing going on with me and Lucious!"

"Not yet, but if you get your way . . ."

Venting. Huffing. Puffing.

"Stop fighting! I swear, Cain and Abel never fought the way you girls do," Ma said, coming into the house behind Eve.

"I don't see what you're so mad about, Eve. I did it for

your own good. He's no good. Why can't you get that through your water head?" Al pushed herself up onto her feet.

"We're not doing anything! Nothing! Nothing!" Eve flung her coat across the room. "This is so unfair. How come I have to suffer because Al made a mistake?" Eve turned to face her mother. "Why, Ma? Why? Don't you see how unfair this is?"

Letting out a loud huff, Eve spun around, turning to leave. She immediately felt a sharp pain between her shoulder blades. A slap. Had Ma gone from yelling to punching?

But the blow hadn't come from Ma. Al stood behind Eve and when Eve turned to face her, she saw Al's face blackened by rage.

"Unfair! You think your life is unfair! Look at me, Eve. Look at me. I'm sick all the time. I can't sleep. I have to pee every fifteen seconds. Do you think that's fair? I didn't want this to happen, but it did. I'm not the one who has been trying to unlock the mystery of girls and boys since she got her first Ken and Barbie. I'm not the one who came home in second grade and announced she had two husbands and two boyfriends." Al grasped her large belly in her hands. "I was the smart one. The practical one. This was not supposed to happen. Not to me."

"Then who was it supposed to happen to . . . *me*?"

Silence. Eve looked from Al to Ma, then, between clenched teeth, she said, "Both of you, both of you would accept this so much better if it had happened to me, wouldn't you? So what, I like boys. I've always liked boys. What does that mean? I'm always, always trying to prove how good a person I am. Al, you're always ragging on me about being so goody-goody. But when it comes down to it, nothing I'll ever do will make either one of you see me any way other than how you want to see me."

"That's because your whole personality, your goody-goody routine, is an act and we can all see that!" Al shot back. "You're pretending to be all sweet and innocent. You're acting. Stop acting, Eve!"

Eve took a half step toward her sister. In a level voice she said, "I'm not the only one around here who's acting. You're acting, too. You're acting like you're better than me, smarter than me. It's killing you knowing that you've made the kind of mistake nobody'd expect of a 'genius' like you. And you're treating me like . . . like I don't care how being pregnant affects you. It hurts, Al. It hurts that you're treating me like I don't care about you." Eve's voice broke, and she looked away, afraid she might break down.

Several seconds passed, and no one said a word. With a shuddering intake of breath, Eve turned to her mother and said, "Why, Ma? Why was it so important for you to push us apart?"

"You can't mean such a cruel thing—you can't!" Ma wailed, sinking down to the sofa. She was the model picture of misery and pain. "I never wanted to drive you girls apart. I only wanted you each to find your own identity and lead your own life. How can you accuse me of such a hurtful thing?"

Eve felt waves of sickness wash over her. Glaring at Al, she yelled, "Lucious isn't the father of your baby, is he?"

Air as thick as rope twisted between the sisters, taut from the invisible force that was pushing them away from one another.

Ma sprang from the sofa. She stepped between them, her eyes dark with fear. "Lucious? Lucious Prior? That little delinquent down at the market? Don't be ridiculous, Eve. Just because you're gaga over him, don't point him at your sister."

Eve felt glued to the floor. Al's eyes narrowed when she spoke. "I'm not you, Eve. He's your fantasy. You're the one who's crazy about him," Al said.

"Then why do you care so much if I'm interested in him?" The muscles in Eve's face had grown so tight, her cheeks and temples ached.

"Because I know you're playing with fire. I'm trying to help you!" Al screamed back.

"So . . ." Eve gulped, "Lucious and you . . ."

"There is no 'Lucious and me, Eve.' There is no Lucious and me!"

Ma's voice was almost pleading as she said, "You know your sister wouldn't get mixed up with a boy like that. You know better, Eve. You know better."

Scene Three

Maybe fifteen minutes had passed. Maybe two hours. Eve was sitting in the hallway outside Lucious's tiny, second-floor apartment. When he came up the stairs, the tears in her eyes were glistening.

"Eve?"

He fumbled for his key and opened the door. Eve alternated between sniffling and burying her face in her hands, muffling her words. It took a while, but Lucious got the gist of it. Eve's sister and mother were accusing her of fooling around. With him.

"I've always tried to be good, better than good, and look where it's gotten me. They don't trust me. I make almost straight A's, but Al is a little genius, skipping a grade, so they treat me like I'm an airhead. An airhead and a slut. I can't take it anymore; I can't!"

It was her big scene, Eve's, and what she imagined would be her first, true, love scene. She was tired of playing the heartsick ingenue. Now she wanted a role with meat. She was Demi Moore in *Ghost*, trembling with sadness and longing as her dead husband's spirit caressed her bare arms.

Eve had decided on the walk over that, whatever happened, happened. She would let it happen naturally, romantically. It wouldn't be as if she'd planned it or anything. If they were together, it would happen because they were desperate for each other, needed each other. The way it happened on soap operas or big-budget movies.

She would be distraught, unable to stop her crying and her anger. Lucious would reach out to comfort her. He would maybe touch her hair, her face, gently kiss the tears on her cheeks. She would whisper muffled words against his chest and neck. She would pull back, saying maybe they shouldn't let things get out of hand. But Lucious—hot, passionate, Lucious—would refuse to let her go. Then he would light candles, play soft music. He would make love to her slowly and whisper, "I love you" in the dark.

Of course that did not happen.

"Eve, Shorty, look, I know you're upset and all, but a brotha' like me needs some rest. Can I call you later?" He yawned.

Eve stopped mid-sniffle. Here she was in the midst of her first love scene, and he was yawning. Did he *not* know his lines, his role?

"Lucious, I need you. I thought we could . . . well . . ." she let her coat fall open and awkwardly pushed herself against him.

She waited.

And waited.

Nothing.

They just stood there, propped against one another for a moment, breathing in and out, in and out.

"Eve . . ."

"Forget it. Just forget it! Am I so ugly, so disgusting, that you can't put your hands on me? Have I been reduced to begging? I thought you liked me. You kissed me and acted like . . . like . . ."

"Like what?" Lucious said evenly.

Eve pushed him away. "Just forget it! I don't need this drama, and I don't need you!"

Lucious pushed her back, though not nearly as hard. He took Eve by the arm and shoved her gently against the wall.

"You're the one bringing drama, so don't pin that on me."

"But Lucious . . ."

"But what? Eve, what did you think would happen today?"

I thought you'd pull me into your arms and make mad, passionate love to me.

Her words came out half whining, half screaming. "Why are you doing this to me?"

"Look, Eve, I told you; I'm working two jobs; I've got a lot of responsibilities going on in my life. I'm going nuts waiting to hear back from this art school in New York. I can't be getting messed up in anybody's little schemes. All right?"

Eve felt shaken. She took a step backwards. The anger that had filled her drained. Eve was being forced to look at a new script, but she couldn't figure out what the next scene should be. She had been fantasizing about Lucious since she hit puberty. Now he was turning her down flat.

"I'll go," she whispered. She squeezed past him, reached for the door.

"Eve . . ."

"I'm sorry," she said. And she meant it, too. She felt ashamed. Not because she'd wanted to have sex without really being in love. Looking at his face, she realized she was seeing his eyes for the first time. He was tired. He looked exhausted.

"Go home, Eve. Let me get some rest. I'll give you a holler later. If it's cool, maybe we can hang out, grab a bite to eat."

Eve nodded as she stepped over the threshold and back into the cramped hallway. She could feel him watching her from the top of the stairs, but she never looked back.

Scene Four

Scene Four

Lucious called Eve's secret cell phone, the one he'd given her, around seven or so, and asked her to come over. Too drained to make up a lie, Eve went to her mother and father and told them the truth. Well, the almost truth. She wanted to have pizza and watch a movie with a friend.

Which is how Eve wound up on the floor at Lucious's apartment watching *Romeo Must Die* and eating pizza.

"Still hard to believe Aaliyah is dead," Lucious said of the beautiful pop star turned movie star on the screen. Eve nodded. One of her favorite fantasies was that she would follow in the path of singer Aaliyah. Her singing talent would launch her acting career. Not that Eve was a great singer, but she'd sung in the church choir, and she wasn't bad.

"Yo, Eve, look . . . about what happened earlier," Lucious began. Eve froze. If he was going to reject her some more, she really didn't think she could take it.

She sat on her heels and brushed crust crumbs off her jeans. "Maybe I should go."

"No, no, no . . . don't go. Listen, I was out of line, all right? I shouldn't have gone off on you like that. I was tired. I apologize."

Eve nodded. So much had changed since the afternoon. His rejection had stung so deeply that she'd vowed she'd never think about sex or boys or boys and sex ever again. And so far, in the last three hours, she'd been true to her word.

"Well, I'm sorry, too. I was upset, and I dumped my problem all over you," she said.

"So don't go." Lucious tugged her hand.

She stayed. They watched the movie. They ate pizza. They . . . Talked. Talked all through the end of the picture. Lucious confided that he was concerned about his grandmother in the retirement home. He confided that he didn't think she had that much more living to do.

"If she dies I'll be all alone." He sighed. "Well, just about alone. Anyway, I don't have much of a family."

"You've got a brother and sister in Georgia, right?"

"We're not close, though. Couldn't tell you the last time I've been down there."

Then they switched gears and talked about the play. Eve confided that Erick Ross kept a thick roll of Life

Savers in his front pants pocket, and whenever she had to press against him as Abigail, she'd feel his minty bulge on her thigh.

They hooted and squealed and talked some more about Lucious preparing a series of sketches he called Vantage Point, which showed the same person from various angles. Eve talked about acing Mr. Harris's latest quiz, learning to ride horses when she was a very little girl, and how frightened she got sometimes when her father left for a long road trip in his rig.

"Sometimes I get this awful feeling, like he might not come back. Like something might happen."

They both sat silent. Then they talked about Lucious's father and how he had left one night and had never come back. Lucious had already lived through the loss of a parent.

Eve stood. "I think I really should be leaving this time," she said. The movie had finished rewinding. Lucious hit the remote, and the digital radio crooned from the television's blue screen.

"This is a beautiful song," Eve said.

Lucious stood. "May I have this dance?" He bowed low and deeply. Eve did her best curtsy, then Lucious pulled her close.

"Eve?"

Then it started again. The tears. Only this time they

weren't the beautiful, picture-perfect tears she'd shed earlier. Now she was sobbing and snorting and making noises that were quite unpleasant and unsuitable for any love scene. She was scared. Scared of being so close to him, scared of her feelings, and scared of feeling stupid so often.

Maybe I'm retarded and should be kept in a small home on the outskirts of town.

"Why're you crying, Eve?"

In keeping with the unromantic and unbeautiful setting, Eve snorted again and wiped her weepy eyes and nose across her sleeve. As if things were not bad enough, Eve began talking, which was dangerous for Eve because unless she rehearsed, she tended to babble and hiccup.

"Maybe I'm a fiend. I think I have some sort of—hiccup—problem. Sex." She babbled and hiccuped.

"Huh?" Lucious began rocking back and forth with her in his arms.

"I came over this afternoon, but I shouldn't have. I thought we would, but we didn't; and you were right to say no, totally right because we shouldn't have. But I have these fantasies, and maybe I'm a fiend 'cause I think about, you know, *it*, a lot, and maybe something's wrong with me."

Eve hadn't realized it, but Lucious was rubbing the

side of her face with his thumb and looking at her intently. Then a long, slow grin spread across his face.

"Ooooooooh, I get it. You wanted to go to bed with me this afternoon."

Abruptly she pulled away. "NO!"

He tugged her back into his arms. "You didn't?" he whispered.

"No, no, no . . . well, I just thought that . . ."

"What?"

"Why are you making this so hard?"

"Miss Eve, I want you to say what's on your mind. What did you think would happen when you came over this afternoon?"

He maintained a sly grin that soon got the better of her. She smiled slyly as well. "Uh, you know. I thought maybe you'd want me to, um, well. Anyway, I thought maybe if you wanted to we could . . ."

"Have sex? Make love? Do the nasty? So you wanted to, but you wanted me to make the moves, right? That way, you wouldn't have to be responsible. Could tell yourself 'Lucious the Experienced' took advantage of you." His words stung like an ice shower. "I don't have any condoms here, Eve."

"I'm on the pill. The doctor tried to get me to wear some sort of patch, but I mean, really. A patch? That is just so gross."

"So when did you start, the pill, I mean?"

"Today!"

His laughter, deep and heartfelt, hurt more than a thousand rejections, a chorus of boos. "You're a trip, Eve." He laughed.

"Forget it! I'm sorry I bothered you!" Her face was hot and her eyes so full of steam she couldn't see straight. She tried to leave, but he blocked the door.

"Get out of my way!" she growled, pushing at his chest.

He didn't even raise his hands, just sort of butted her with his body. "You stop," he said.

Now they were in a strange pushing match—she with her hands, he with his body. The language of their touching went silent, and another love song wailed from the digital radio. That was when he kissed her, slow and hard.

THUD!

The outer rim of his fist hit the wall above her head. "You're messing up my head, Shorty," Lucious said.

Eve, for her part, was going in a hundred different directions, fearing she'd forgotten some basic things like how to talk or walk or exit stage right.

His voice rasped, "I told you I don't have any condoms."

"But I . . ."

"Look, Shorty, I know your doctor told you the pill takes a little while to kick in, right?" She nodded. The doctor had said something like that, not that she was paying attention. Back at the doctor's office, she vowed to remain a virgin until her mid-eighties just to spite her mother.

Now she was trembling, and it wasn't an act. Had she come to Lucious because she loved him and was ready to be with him, or because she wanted to prove some kind of point? His hand slid around her waist.

"I just keep having all these questions, all these feelings. I want to, then I don't, you know?" she said.

He kissed her neck. "I think I know something we can do that will ease some of your stress and keep us both out of trouble."

For a brief moment, Eve thought he might've rented a copy of *Dirty Dancing* because *Dirty Dancing* was always an excellent sexual-stress reliever for her. However, when she felt his fingers on her zipper and felt his thumbs urging her jeans into a denim puddle, she decided that Lucious wasn't having a Blockbuster moment.

"Um, Lucious . . ." Shouldn't she say something? Shouldn't she do something?

But what?

Eve couldn't even decide if she really wanted it to

happen. Was this how she'd pictured her first time? An ad for Viagra blared on the radio. Not sexy, just pathetic.

"Lucious, Lucious, I . . ." she couldn't speak without tiny gasps. He was kissing her navel, the line above her panties, then her thigh.

"When is your birthday, Eve?"

She couldn't handle the tough questions. "I don't know," she said, her mind clouded.

"Don't worry, just consider this as your gift. The safest sex you can have. Can't get pregnant. Can't catch anything. And if I do it right, it should make you feel real good."

Then he kissed her thigh again, and again, and again, moving up, up, up until . . .

Omigoodness! Not *Dirty Dancing*. It was *American Pie*, maybe *American Pie 2*.

When he was done, Lucious left a trail of wet kisses up her body and lay beside Eve on the floor. Eve's body tingled with electricity. She'd bitten her fist to muffle the cry that seemed to creep out of nowhere and threatened to drown out the litany of Viagra ads that blurted from the radio in between songs. At least they weren't as bad as the ads about AIDS. Lucious had kept his promise; with his lips, his tongue, his playful bite, he'd made her body feel alive.

Her heart, however, was doing something weird.

Something she couldn't quite figure. Her heart made it hard for her to look him in the eye or smile or replay it over and over in her mind. He had put his mouth on her—down there. It was . . . She squirmed. It was so much more intimate, so much more personal to be with him like that. It was a lot different than she had imagined. In the fantasies it'd always been so perfect. In the fantasies she'd never pictured herself naked from the waist down, looking for her underwear on the floor and feeling all squirmy. She dressed quickly. She was ready to go.

Scene Five

He was breathless.

"I think I'm going to get in," Lucious practically yelled into the phone. Eve stood cradling the phone against her ear in the hallway at school.

"Man, this is it. I know it. I'm going to get this scholarship, and then I'm outta here," he said. Eve knew he was talking about the school project in New York, where he'd submitted his portfolio. She pictured his face filled with pride, dark eyes shimmering. She wished she were near enough to hold him.

"I'll keep everything I have crossed, my fingers, my toes, everything, until you know for sure," Eve said.

"I gotta go, but I just wanted to tell you."

Eve returned to the rehearsal and delivered her greatest interpretation of Abigail to date. Even Joel said so.

"I'm very impressed with how well you're doing, Eve. Our production will be outstanding, and you're one of the reasons why."

Eve thanked him and followed her fellow cast members into the wings. Bethany complained about aching feet, and Amanda Woods—the girl playing Elizabeth Proctor—rubbed her lower back. Eve looked forward to going home and thinking about Lucious, his phone call, their first kiss. Time was flying past, she thought, and she was eager for each new day. She had a grand plan. First, Lucious was going to get his scholarship and head for New York. Second, she was going to be a smash in the school play.

Third, she was going to win one of the summer-stock scholarships and join Lucious in New York for the experience of a lifetime.

Eve started toward the telephone to call her mother and ask if she'd pick her up, but decided instead to walk home and enjoy the crisp night air.

Clash!

"Ow!" cried Eve. She'd walked right into . . . Al?

"Hey, are you all right?" Eve said, rubbing the bruised spot on her forehead and looking down at Al's belly.

Al was holding something in her hand. Her eyes were fierce and dark. She thrust the small sheet of paper at Eve. "How did you get this? How?" She was holding the miniature portrait Lucious had drawn of Eve. "Lucious drew this!"

"How did *you* get it?" Eve asked.

Al flung the drawing at Eve. It fluttered toward the floor like smudged confetti.

"Stop it! That's mine!" Eve snatched it from the air before it could hit the floor.

"Yours!" Al was practically shouting.

Now it was Eve's turn to thrust the small portrait into Al's face. "Look. Of course it's mine. How do you know Lucious drew it? Why do you care?" Eve noticed that they were both panting with anger or maybe frustration. Al squinted, taking in all the details of the drawing. Her eyes widened and her mouth made a tiny *o*, but she kept quiet.

"You didn't think it was of you, did you?"

"Don't be stupid," Al snapped. "It must have fallen out of your stupid bag in Mr. Harris's room. He saw me in the hall a little while ago and gave it to me."

Eve shrugged. "So what's the problem?" She tucked the small portrait inside her notebook.

"The problem is that Lucious is known for making these miniatures, especially for the girls he's messing around with. You just can't leave him alone. What's it going to take?"

"I've never heard of him making these portraits for anybody else." Eve sounded defensive.

"Trust me; it's not a secret."

They glared at one another. Finally Al shook her

head and let out a long sigh. "You have no idea what you're playing with, but you're going to get burned, Eve."

Eve felt her fist clench at her side. "If you're so worried about somebody getting burned, Al, maybe *you* should stay away from Lucious. And stay away from me, too!"

Eve worked to release the tension in her face and neck as she walked hurriedly to Lucious's place. Al was driving her nuts. Eve was still desperate to have her twin back in her life again, but it seemed as if they couldn't talk to one another without some sort of explosion. Maybe Lucious wasn't the problem, Eve thought. Maybe the problem was that Al hated her so much, they'd be at each other's throats no matter what they talked about.

A zillion brilliant, silver stars glittered above the market, making the slushy street glow. Eve saw Lucious's truck parked along the curb. He was there, too, along with a few friends. As she crossed the street, he looked up and saw her, then beckoned to her to hurry.

"Come give Big Daddy a hug!" Lucious called out. His voice was loud and a little slurred. He was standing on the flat bed of the truck along with another boy. Lucious tipped a bottle to his lips and passed it to a boy with snow-white hair and cocoa brown skin.

"I did it! I did it!" Lucious was yelling and doing a goofy jig. He jumped down from the truck, stumbled a little, then picked Eve up and twirled her around. His grip was too tight; his arms bit into her sides.

"They told me I wouldn't make it, Baby Girl. They told me I wasn't nothing, all those teachers, s'posed to be smart. They can kiss my . . ."

"Put me down, Lucious. Let's walk to your place," Eve cut in. When he slid her back to the ground, she hooked her arm in his.

The snowy-haired boy held the paper-bag-wrapped bottle toward Lucious. "Want any more of this, man?"

Eve tensed. She was shocked to see Lucious drinking anything after the talks they'd had about how he "used to be" wild, but his wild days were in the past.

"Naw, man, you go on, knock that out. You see I'm with my lady," said Lucious.

My lady.

So when he's sober he has morals, but drunk I'm his lady!

Eve tried not to bristle as she guided him along the slick pavement.

The walk to his place should have taken less than five minutes, but because Lucious was wobbling and stopping to pee behind trees, it took them almost half an hour. By the time they climbed the stairs and entered the apartment, Lucious fell face first onto the sofa. He whispered, "Please don't leave me. Please?" Eve peeled off her coat and went to the phone. Lucious was asleep before Eve's call could go through.

"Um, Ma, it's me. I'm . . . studying with Bethany. I'll see you later." Her lie lingered in the silence, and Lucious never stirred.

It was ten o'clock when Lucious awoke. Eve was sitting on the floor, a pillow under her legs. She had abandoned reading her homework assignment after she'd switched to Showtime right in the middle of *Armageddon. Armageddon.* Man, the signs just didn't seem to stop. The sexy, young movie astronaut was looking grim when Eve heard Lucious stir on the sofa.

"What?" Lucious flinched when he saw her, then sat up like his head was filled with water. Eve remembered the slumber party she'd gone to as a freshman. That night, after some of the girls were sleeping, a few of the more adventurous ones had gotten into the parents' liquor. Eve was right there with them, sipping and burping and trying to feel grownup.

The next morning her head felt awful, and her stomach felt worse. Lucious didn't look nearly as bad as she had felt that time, but he did look disoriented.

"Man, I had a buzz," Lucious said, excusing himself and going into the bathroom. Again.

When he came out, he asked, "Where does your moms think you're at?"

"Bethany's, but I told her I'd be home before eleven. She and my father are out, so they won't be home when I get back anyway."

Lucious had a sheepish expression. He cast his eyes downward. "I feel like I swallowed a pillow," he said. "Let me get my coat, and I'll walk with you. I could use the air."

They put on their winter gear, and Lucious held the door open. Outside the temperature had dropped, and both Lucious and Eve huddled deep inside their coats. They'd gone two blocks before Lucious spoke.

"I got a little crazy today, Shorty. Don't think I'm wild or nothing like that. I've had a lot on my mind, a lot to sort out." He stopped moving and stared at her. Eve felt her cheeks flushing as pink as brown skin would allow.

"What?" she finally said.

He leaned over, kissed the tip of her nose, and smiled. "I was just thinking. I wish things could have been different with us. You know, the timing and all. It wasn't supposed to happen this way."

Eve felt as though she were floating away. He looked so sincere. She changed the subject. "When do you think you'll leave?"

"Oh, it won't be for a while. Classes begin in July—so June, maybe."

Eve looked up. A star shot across the sky, leaving a foamy trail. Another sign!

As if he'd seen it, too, Lucious reached out and clasped Eve's hand. Her heart hummed. With all that was happening in her life—the play, the fights with Al, and now Lucious—Eve believed New York was more than a dream; it was a necessity. It had to be more than a coincidence that the boy she'd loved from afar for years wanted to live in the same city she'd visited in her fantasies a million times.

When they were a block away from her house, Eve slowed. She did not want to risk bumping into her parents if they decided to come home early. "I think this is far enough," she said. Her voice caught in her throat, surprising her. When Lucious spoke, the softness of his voice was a surprise as well.

"Thanks for what you did today. Staying with me, making sure I was all right," Lucious said. They faced one another. Eve met his gaze, and when he bent his neck, she rose to her toes.

The kiss was slow and sensuous. He kissed first her lips, one at a time, then used his tongue to part her lips, kissing her mouth again and again. When car tires crunched on the frozen ground beyond them, Eve felt him pull away. She felt the intrusion of ice-cold air replacing the warmth of his body. She was panting, and the panting made her feel embarrassed.

"Well," Lucious said, "I'd better let you get going. I'll wait till you get to your house." Eve didn't try to speak, because she wasn't sure she could. She nodded, gave him a sort of shoulder bump, then did a skip-hop-run across the street and up the block.

When she reached her front porch, Eve peered back in the direction from which she had come. After a second or two, she saw a shadow step beneath a streetlight and wave. She waved back, then put her key in the lock. Eve was still panting, partly from running, but mostly from the kiss—when she closed the front door and began removing her boots.

Scene Seven

Scene Seven

His taste, sweet and salty, lingered, his voice still soft against her ear. Eve rolled onto her side in the bed facing the window, the cell phone to her ear.

"I can't stop thinking about you," she said, feeling like the star of her own love story.

"Me, too," Lucious murmured into the phone.

"Lucious," she whispered. Her hand found the spot that she was seeking. She stifled a moan.

"I know what you're doing," Lucious said.

"No," Eve replied, her fingers stopping. Was it right to admit something so personal? Then she remembered what had happened a few weeks earlier. Him kissing her thigh and moving higher and higher until he touched his tongue to her body's most private part. She shivered.

"Don't be embarrassed. I do it. If I was there, though, neither one of us would have to. We could, you know, help each other out."

Eve dropped her head back against the pillow. "I have to go," she rasped.

"Me, too," Lucious said.

They hung up after making promises to get together later in the week. A tear bubbled in the well of Eve's eye—pure, watery joy. She whisked it away, and her lips curled into a smile.

Act Eight

Scene One

*The grizzly bear charged through the thicket of trees
and found Eve helpless in a circle of icy moonlight. The
moonlight grew more and more silvery until it pooled
up, no longer flat, turning to water. Eve sloshed in
water up to her ankles, her screams trapped behind the
mask she wore, an egg-yolk yellow happy face. The egg
face smiled at the grizzly and held out its arms. Eve's
arms. The animal charged, crashing through the grass
and splashing through the water. A scream echoed in
Eve's head, gut-wrenching and fierce. The sound
bounced off the trees and sliced through Eve's body
more sharply than the bear's flesh-ripping claws.*

Eve didn't know when she first woke up or when the
beating began. Her head felt fuzzy, and her mind
wouldn't focus. Moonlit shadows broke apart in tiny
pieces. Movement. She was being slapped across her
back. She was being shaken. Was it the grizzly? Voices,
shrill and loud, slashed the night apart.

"You lying little harlot! Liar!" Ma bent over Eve's sleep-drugged body. Ma's coat always smelled like the peppermints she kept in her pocket. Her face was beyond angry.

"Ruthie, please!" Daddy's voice boomed.

Eve tried to kick her legs free from the tangle of blankets, but her limbs felt useless.

"Stop protecting her. She's been lying to us from the get-go. 'I'm at play practice, Ma. I'm at Bethany's, Ma.'"

Eve, wincing from the blows, had slid onto the floor, too shocked to breathe normally. Daddy was pulling Ma away.

"Belly, where you been tonight? We saw Bethany with her mama and daddy, and Al says a boy brought you home. Where were you, Belly?" Daddy's voice was as soft as Daddy's voice could get.

Eve thought her father earnestly believed she had a good explanation. That hurt Eve more than being slapped.

"I . . . I just needed some time to myself," she lied.

"Stop it! Stop it! Stop it!" Ma yelled, lunging toward Eve. Daddy grabbed Ma's arm, but her voice, already shrill, continued to rise. "Stop lying. You're always lying. I can't take it anymore. And since you want to be so deceitful, you can forget about that damned play. Forget it!"

Eve began sobbing. Her mouth opened and she gasped, "Please, Ma, please."

Ma was sobbing as well. "I knew it. I knew you'd wind up messing up. Pregnant and in high school, with no future. I knew it. I knew it."

The rasping of sharp, tearful breathing filled the room. Eve struggled to get the words out. "Ma, I'm not the one who got pregnant. I'm so sorry about Al, Ma, but I haven't done anything wrong."

Ma sank to the floor, her rage gone. Eve wanted to reach out to her, yet the thought of touching her mother made her recoil.

Daddy began stroking Ruth Ann's neck, and her mother's ragged breathing slowed.

When Ma raised her head, her eyes were glassy with tears. "You're right. You're right. She messed up, but I've messed up, too. I messed up everything that mattered to your grandma Peaches. I just wanted to raise daughters my mama could be proud of. Daughters who weren't like . . . *me*." She dropped her head, mumbling, "Mama told me not to sleep with Jonathan. I didn't listen. I thought he'd marry me. A few weeks. . . . That's all it lasted." Daddy helped her to her feet and led her down the hall.

Eve sat in a tangle of sheets and blankets on the floor, gulping air and struggling to slow her own ragged breathing. All the while she kept her eyes glued to the door across the hall. Al's door. It never opened, not even a crack. Eve felt her lips tighten into a hard line.

Forgiveness. Eve had been praying for it since the year before. No more. Eve pushed herself to a standing position, grabbed hold of her bedroom door, then slammed it shut as hard as she could. She wasn't begging for forgiveness anymore from Al or Ma.

To hell with Al, Eve sneered. To hell with her and Ma.

Scene Two
Scene Two

Before eight the next morning, Eve was seated beside her father. He had suggested it might be best if she went to Aunt Mary's for a few days till things cooled down.

Eve hadn't questioned him. She'd simply packed a bag and followed her father into the kitchen for coffee, then out the door.

A few days later, on Sunday, Eve sat in church between Aunt Mary's friend, Cally, and her aunt, feeling numb. When Cally squeezed Eve's fingers, Eve felt the sharp impression of the woman's gleaming wedding and engagement rings.

Cally squeezed her fingers again, and Eve glanced at the woman's face. As if Eve didn't have enough reasons to hate herself, she added being selfish to the list. Here she was crying for her wretched self, and Cally was graciously grieving the loss of her baby. Miscarriage. The perfectly round belly that had sent Ma and Al cowering at Aunt Mary's at Christmas now lay flat and empty.

Back at Aunt Mary's after the church service, Cally said, "Mary told me a little bit about the problems between you and your mother. Wanna talk about it?"

Eve shrugged. "I'm not messing around. . . ." Her voice trailed off. Remembering Lucious with his tongue and lips touching her most private places made her blush. She swallowed hard and said, "I love him. We haven't done anything wrong." Now Eve was sobbing.

Aunt Mary sat beside Eve on the sofa and wrapped her arm around Eve's shoulder.

Cally said, "My grandmother was always convinced I was going to be 'hot in the pants.' That's what she called liking boys. From the time I entered grade school, all I ever heard about was how dangerous it was for a girl to get 'hot in the pants.' By middle school I refused to wear pants. Only dresses, because I was afraid if I wore them—pants, I mean—I'd end up too hot, and Lord only knows what would happen then."

The three of them laughed, deep-down, good-feeling laughter. It was the first time in days Eve had felt like laughing. Cally's laughter stopped just short of her eyes. "My granny died two years ago, just before I married Tom. I think she went to her grave fearing that if I made one wrong move, I'd end up destroyed, all because of getting hot in the pants."

Eve thought of Grandma Peaches and looked away.

She didn't feel like laughing anymore. When the door-bell rang, Eve hoped it signaled a change of subject. It did . . . and it didn't.

Daddy came in holding his hat and mumbling some-thing about how nice a day it was. Eve could smell a mixture of sunshine and turpentine on his clothes. He'd probably been at his old workshop.

"Belly, Mama is so sorry, about everything," Daddy said, his voice a husky whisper.

Aunt Mary cut in, her voice rich and important sounding. "Mothers and daughters often reach a diffi-cult point in their relationship where they must re-eval-uate their roles. I believe Twin and her mother have reached that point."

Eve smiled despite herself. Aunt Mary sounded as though she were in court laying a foundation for a case.

Daddy sank down on the sofa beside Eve. He was still holding his hat, twirling it as he did when he was anx-ious or nervous. His back was ramrod straight, as always. Eve slid closer to her father and dropped her head onto her father's knee.

"Oh, Daddy, you have to make Ma let me be in the play. I have an important role, and I can't let everybody down. I'm sorry. Sorry about everything."

Her father patted her head. "There, there. Mama will let you back in the play, Belly, I'll speak to her. She's just hurting inside, hurting real bad over this thing with Al. She just isn't herself." Daddy's voice left an exhausted trail, as thick and puffy as skywriting.

Eve pulled herself upright. She had another performance to give. "Daddy, nothing happened between Lucious and me. I mean, I . . . I love him, but we didn't do anything bad. I haven't been bad, Daddy."

"Yes, Belly, yes . . ."

"I guess I wanted to know what it was like. To fall in love and be in love forever. Ma gets to spend her life with the man of her dreams. I just wanted to know what that was like for . . . a little while, I guess." Eve hugged her father around the neck. Oh, of course she knew that Johnny B. was supposed to be the love of her mother's life, but she was putting on a big show for her father's sake. She was acting—and lying.

And it made her feel good.

Daddy stood and Eve stood, too. Daddy looked at Eve and said, "See, that's just the thing, Belly. I love your mama more than the air I breathe. But you've heard enough of the talk to know I'm not the love of her life. But I'll spend the rest of my life trying to make what I have good enough."

Daddy's words crackled in the den, and when Eve met his gaze, she wanted to cringe. He wasn't acting. He was intense and sincere, and—as good as her little act had

been—it paled beside her father's sober honesty. What
was worse, she could see in his eyes that he knew exactly what she had been trying to do.

Eve looked away, wanting to feel ashamed. Wanting
to beg for forgiveness.

Forgiveness. There it was again. Well, she wasn't
looking for forgiveness anymore. Not ever again.

Scene Three

Scene Three

Blueberry muffins sat on the counter, and the scent of hot, brewing coffee filled every corner of the kitchen. Eve had awakened before everyone else and decided to get breakfast started. She told herself she wasn't doing it to impress anybody; she just wanted blueberry muffins.

Her father was the first to come in. He kissed the top of her head, poured some coffee, and placed a muffin on a saucer. He opened the back door and scooped up the newspaper. "Dress warm today, Belly. I don't care what the calendar says; winter's not quite through with us yet," he said.

Eve bristled. Weather. He was talking about the damned, stupid, freaking weather again. She gripped the ladle she'd dipped into the pancake batter. She sighed with frustration. She wasn't mad at the weather or her father for talking about the weather. She was just . . . fed up.

As if on cue, the kitchen doors swung open. Ma walked in dressed immaculately in a starched, white blouse and a knee-length, navy blue skirt and carrying a matching blue blazer over her arm. Whenever Ma and Eve had been in the same room since the big blowup, tension filled the space around them.

Eve felt her spine stiffen. She clenched her jaws with such force, her face hurt. Eve wanted to pour the pancake batter into the now-sizzling frying pan, but when she lifted the bowl the batter swished around and she had to lower it again.

Ma poured herself a cup of coffee. She looked at Daddy and said, "I know you didn't make this, because it's delicious." She'd tried to make her tone playful.

Daddy looked up with a too-wide grin. "Not me, Sugar. Your baby over there did it."

Eve refused to turn and face her mother, but she slid her eyes to one side in grudging acknowledgment of Ma's presence. Ma took another sip, then she cleared her throat.

"If you need to practice extra from here on out, don't worry about working those few days a week down at the firm. You can still work, of course, if you want, but it's not necessary." Ma cleared her throat again, then looked away.

Eve stared straight ahead at the tile backsplash

behind the stove. Again she gripped the ladle, torn between the urge to pour the batter into the pan and the urge to fling it onto her mother's pressed, white shirt.

She did neither. Her father was too honest and straightforward to appreciate an act right now, but she knew her mother expected nothing less than a performance.

"Thanks, Ma. I'll check with Joel," Eve said, giving her mother the briefest glance.

The three of them, Eve, Ma, and Daddy, remained frozen in that breakfast scene for several minutes. Eve resented feeling like her mother was just showing off by letting her know she'd had the power to stop Eve from participating in the play. Finally Eve plopped some pancake batter into the frying pan. It landed with a sizzle.

When Eve made herself look around, at last, she saw her mother had sat down at the table across from Daddy. Ma was looking at Eve, too. When their eyes met, they both looked away. Eve didn't say another word. She felt angry and off balance. She felt like throwing open the kitchen door and running for her life.

Scene Four

Scene Four

Eve recalled the pain of her mother's attack, recalled the isolation of her brief exile, even though it had happened more than two weeks before. Now she was rehearsing the play and drawing on the painful memory to help her with a scene. Before Ma's assault, Eve could only imagine the hurt of being shunned by an entire village, like Abigail Williams.

Now, of course, Eve felt she understood the scene better. It was the scene where the church elders, who had been Abigail's biggest supporters, turned their backs. Eve got this round, heavy feeling in her gut and had a hard time swallowing. Abigail would have felt terrified, would have felt almost dead if she'd gone from having the townspeople hang on every word, to having them look at her like some sort of lying freak.

"You are really doing a fantastic job with this role," Joel encouraged Eve after the rehearsal. Bethany nodded in agreement.

"Girl, you were really feeling it today."

The heavy feeling in the pit of Eve's stomach remained. She formed what she hoped wasn't a sick-looking smile and said, "Life really is the best teacher." She instinctively rubbed the spot on her neck where her locket, the one matching Al's, had hung. After what Eve saw as her sister's final betrayal, she had removed the locket and stuffed it in her book bag.

The next night Joel said, "Your performances are getting so strong, Eve. You're really developing a powerful presence." She wondered if that meant she was getting closer to the real Eve, or farther away.

Scene Five

Scene Five

The play opened on a Thursday night, the third week of April.

Several cast members showed up green with stage-fright fever. Eve sat at the dressing table, her long, dark hair pulled back in a ponytail and her fluffy, white bonnet tied under her chin. She wore a lace-up corset over her blouse, which accentuated the curve of her bosom. In the mirror she looked innocent, but at the same time, with the curves and the sly smile, she looked mature. Sensual. Feeling that way made her feel strangely calm, and powerful. Like Abigail.

On opening night her family and friends came to the play. Even Eugenia and the boys were there. Everyone sat together in a cluster in the third row to the right of the stage.

In the first act, in the middle of one of Abigail's big speeches—"... *Let either of you breathe a word, or the edge of a word about the other things, and I will come to you in the black of some terrible night and I will bring a pointy reckoning that will shudder you . . .*"— that's when Eve felt it. Pure electricity. She wasn't Eve anymore. Just like at rehearsal, she had become Abigail. And she understood something. Underneath all of Abigail's boldness, fear drove her more than passion. The fear of being left behind while John Proctor, Elizabeth, the whole village moved forward in a world with no place for sexual, unmarried girls.

"You were . . . amazing," Al said later, when Daddy took everyone out to Hubbard's for dinner. Eve stared, unable to process the compliment. She sputtered "thank you" and looked away.

Aunt Mary took Eve's face in her hands. "Twin, you've got real talent. I am so proud." Aunt Mary choked up, but Eve felt the pureness of her sincerity and grinned, hugging her aunt with both arms. Aunt Mary's husky voice gusted across the dinner table. "I know you might not believe it, but in my heart, Twin, I can feel your grandma Peaches smiling. She would be so very, very proud!"

Then Eve heard a sound. A wet sound. Part snort, part pain.

Ma.

"Was Mama ever proud of me?" Ruth Ann Noble said. Eve felt the grin on her face freeze as she and the others turned to look at her mother.

The question was so unexpected, everyone at the table—even Benny and Nick and Eugenia—went silent.

"Of course she was proud," Aunt Mary said.

Not on my big night, Ma. Don't take this night away from me!

Eve sat helpless, praying for the numbness to come and protect her from the anger bubbling inside. She'd felt something special up on that stage. In all the times she'd pretended to receive Academy Awards or bowed in the basement thanking her adoring fans, she'd never understood what it would feel like to actually be good at acting. She had, instead, spent her time fantasizing about living the life of an actress.

But tonight she had proved she was good at it. And that felt better than good. It felt right. And now Ma was stealing it away.

Ma made quiet, ladylike sobs, her narrow shoulders going up and down, reminding Eve of a butterfly trapped beneath a net. "Mama never told me she was proud of anything I did. Not ever. I took care of things when she got ill. I was always there for her. But it was like she couldn't even see me," said the wet butterfly.

Daddy quickly moved from his seat beside Eve, where he had been poised to wrap her in yet another of his infamous bear hugs and speak way too loudly about her greatness, and went to sit beside Ma.

Eve sat entranced as she watched the performance. There sat Ma, slumped over, eyes sadder than just about anything, little guppylike breaths of sadness puffing from her lips. And Daddy, the leading man, stroking her back with his large hands, saying soothing words.

Al, who vied for co-star credit, complained that her chair was too hard. Aunt Mary leaned upon her cane to find her friend, the manager of Hubbard's, and ask him to bring "a perfectly plump pillow."

So here Eve was in another play with actors and characters and even stage props. Well, she thought, she would not be part of the audience. Dinner was probably on the table before anyone noticed that she had made a brilliant exit.

Scene Six

Glow Worm slithered to the front of the room. Eve sensed something major was about to happen. Since that awful night at the restaurant, Eve had prayed non-stop for the announcement of the scholarship winners. She was more determined than ever to make a getaway.

"I want you to know we have an announcement of huge significance," said Glow Worm. When she said *significance*, the *s* sound sizzled sideways, lasting forever. "We have our scholarship winners."

Mr. Mann entered the classroom, his arms folded across his chest. Eve focused on the floor, afraid to look up. Two names were read, and squeals and high fives echoed.

". . . and . . ."

Glow Worm sucked in her breath, and Eve felt certain that if the woman did not spit out the third and final name, Eve would fall dead from nerves.

"Eve Noble, or, as I have come to know her, Miss Abigail Williams."

The world stopped spinning, then spun at a crazy pace. Pats on the back, congratulations. Eve saw it all, felt it all, but had the odd sensation that it was all happening to a stranger.

A few days passed, and Eve kept the scholarship news to herself. She wanted to savor it. Al had been getting scholarship and college brochures from all over. University of North Carolina. Howard University. The University of Virginia. Al was getting bigger and bigger, yet Eve noticed she looked as determined as ever to go ahead, have her baby, put it up for adoption, and get the hell out of Eden.

Now, with the performing-arts scholarship to attend the workshop in New York City, Eve felt some of the leaden pressure that had weighed her down for months start to dissipate.

She was going to be free, after all—at least for a little while.

Scene Seven

Eve paused to avoid bumping into Al. They were both pushing through the swinging kitchen doors into the living room. Ma was holding the phone, and Eve realized she hadn't heard it ring.

"...anything about it, but Eve does like to keep secrets," Ma said. Her eyes were hard, and Eve didn't move.

"Well, as I said," Ma went on, her hands moving swatches of quilting fabric across the table. Since Al's pregnancy, Eve noted, Ma had returned to a number of old hobbies inherited from Grandma Peaches, including trying to quilt. Brilliant pieces of cotton fabric—lime calico, golden flowers, pink candy-stripes, cottony-blue clouds—lay side by side on the living-room table. The riot of color seemed to go with the frenetic play between Benny and his scraggly little puppy.

Ma continued, "My husband and I were not aware of any scholarship to New York, but Eve is not going to New York."

Was Eve really hearing her mother right?

"Ma, I was waiting to tell you and Daddy . . ."

Her mother waved her off and shrugged. "You're not going, Eve." Without even waiting for Eve to answer, she turned to Benny.

"Don't worry, Baby, we'll take care of your little dog," Ma said.

"But . . ." Benny whined.

"Go. Aunt Mary's veterinarian friend is coming to look at Jelly Bean. Don't worry; we'll take care of your sick puppy."

Eve's mouth went dry.

"But Ma, let me explain."

"You should have 'explained' from the beginning, then I could have told you it was out of the question."

The voices that usually spoke all at once inside her head, confusing her, quieted. Eve took a step closer. "I'm going," she said.

Ma drew in a sharp breath. "Go if you want to, but you won't be coming back here if you do," she said.

"Go where?" Benny said.

"Mind your business," Ma said.

"Ma, I'm not feeling so well," Al said. She grimaced.

Ma stood. "Too early, Al, you've got two more weeks."

"But Ma, I don't feel well. I feel . . . funny."

Ma reached for Al, placed her finger under Al's chin,

and lifted her face to get a better look at her eyes. Then she placed her hands on Al's neck. "You do feel warm," she said. "Come on, Baby, Mama'll get you comfortable, and you'll be fine."

"I'm going, Ma. I don't care what you say; I'm going." Eve heard herself speak, but the voice was low and urgent and completely unlike her own. Ma held Al by the arm, massaging her neck. She turned to face Eve.

"Get out of my sight for a while, Eve, before you make me do something we'll both regret," she said.

Eve could hear herself breathing. "I am going to accept that scholarship, and I'm going to be a part of that summer theater group, Ma. It lasts for six weeks. Six weeks. What is the problem? I worked hard for this. I have a right to go."

Rigid as a toy soldier, Ma growled, "Get out! Get out of my house. Get out of my sight. If you think you're so grown you can do whatever the hell you want, then go do it."

"Or what?" Eve sneered.

"Eve, you have no respect for me and probably none for yourself. Don't you understand I'm only trying to do what's best for you?"

Eve's lip trembled as tears spurted from her eyes. "Ma, why does it have to be like this?"

"If you can't obey and show me some respect, you

should go. Just go!" Ma repeated.

Eve ran out to the back porch, leaned against the railing, and stared at the pale gray sky.

"Eve," a voice said behind her.

Eve jumped. Al was standing there, her hand in the middle of her back, a sick expression on her face.

"What?" Eve snapped.

"I'm sorry," Al said.

Eve wasn't prepared for her sister's tone, as soft as new rain. What was she up to this time?

"Why, Al? Why did you do this? Why did you let a boy get you pregnant? Why did you ruin everything for me? Telling Ma about me and Lucious, not that there was anything to tell. Why did you do it?"

The wind picked up, and the warm air enveloped Eve. Could Al feel it, too?

"Ma is trippin', just like always. You deserve to use your scholarship," Al said.

"But why, Al? Why do you treat me like I'm an idiot?"

Al closed her eyes. When she opened them, she sighed. "Eve, you play around so damned much. You're always pretending, acting silly. Then, poof, all of a sudden you want to be taken seriously."

"I have a right to act however I want. Ma was in there talking about respect. Well, that's a big ha. Neither of you respects me. Not you or Ma." It shook Eve to hear herself sound so much like Ma had a few moments earlier. "Lucious is my friend, but you couldn't stand that, could you?"

"Have you ever talked to him about my baby?"

Al's question stung like a blow to the face. "What?"

"Look, Eve, I'm pregnant because I thought I was too smart to get caught. Lucious . . ." Al released a bitter laugh.

Eve shook her head.

"He told me I was different, special, and I told myself I was too smart to get played by a delinquent." Al rubbed her tummy.

"Stop it! Stop it! You're lying to me!"

"You're always looking for a sign, Eve. Sometimes you have to do what you know is right. God can't just send you telegrams to keep you out of trouble, no matter how much you want to believe he will." Al eased onto the railing and rested her weight against the wooden column.

"I know I can be flaky sometimes, but that's how everybody expects me to be. Ma doesn't want to know what's really on my mind; she doesn't want to know the kinds of things I'm really thinking about," Eve said.

"Like thinking about Lucious and wondering what it would be like to . . ."

"So what if I do wonder about it? If what you just said was true, I guess I wasn't the only one wondering. Don't worry, Al. I'm not like you. I won't think I'm too smart to do something stupid. You're the smart one, remember?"

"It won't be how you might think," Al said, moving toward the back door. She looked tired. Her belly was huge and looked like the most uncomfortable thing in the world. Then she started to cry. "He thought I was you. He saw the baseball cap I was wearing and thought I was 'the one who wears the silly hats,' and that was why he came on to me. It made me mad that he came on to me thinking I was you, so I thought, what the hell, I'll have some fun with him. But like you said, he's actually kind of nice. I liked the attention, liked how he made me feel. I thought . . ."

"Stop it! Stop lying! You're desperate to make my life miserable!" Eve started to back away. Was Al really so vicious, so hateful, that she'd lie about something so important?

Or worse . . . could it be true?

"I'll bet," Al said, "when Abigail was fooling around with John Proctor, even though he was married, he made her feel as though she was the purest woman in the world. Until what they were doing made her feel like something else."

Eve couldn't think of anything to say but couldn't bear the thought of Al getting the last word. "What do you know about Abigail or the play? You only saw it once."

"But I read it years ago in honors English. I'm the smart one, remember?" Al went inside the kitchen, and Eve stared at her until she disappeared.

Always has to have the last word.

Eve scooped her backpack off the floor. All the emotion that had been swimming around in her body spurred her feet into action, and she began to run.

Tree boughs shook in the rising wind, and thick, fat rain pelted the world. Eve ran with determination, ran against the wind. She knew where she was going.

Scene Eight

Damn Walgreens has to be the brightest drugstore in the universe!

"You're the girl from the play?" the salesclerk asked.

Eve nodded. "How much?" she asked, pushing the box across the scanner.

The clerk was only a few years older than Eve. "It says six ninety-five. You want 'em?" she asked, holding the box of condoms.

Eve nodded. The girl said, "I was at that play, you know, the one you were in. My sister played the little girl who got bewitched or whatever." She handed Eve her change. The sales clerk's name was Joy.

Joy smiled, and Eve picked up the box of condoms. The electronic doors parted, and Eve hunched her shoulders against the rain.

She arrived at Lucious's apartment with an ache in her side from too much running. He opened the door as though he'd been waiting for her. Maybe he had. Eve felt as though she were in her own dream, the one she'd had for so long—where Lucious was the answer to her prayers. He opened the door wide, and she fell inside, safe in his arms.

She raised her head. "Is it true? Are you really the father of Al's baby?"

Rain dripped from her hair, and her wet clothes clung to her body. "Please tell me you aren't! Please! I told her that you'd told me you weren't, but she said it today, said you were the father. She said it just to hurt me, right? Right?"

Eve was nearly hysterical. Lucious held her in his arms and said, "Shh, shh, Baby. Right. It's all right. It's all right . . ."

Eve sobbed after telling Lucious what Al had told her, and Lucious stroked her back, massaging her shoulders.

"Look, I want us to talk about all of this. I'm leaving tomorrow, and I won't have the chance to see you for a while. Right now, though, I have to run down to the store."

She grabbed his shirt. "You're leaving?" Stupid, stupid, stupid.

He looked down. "I have to get down to the market."

"But it's raining," Eve whined. Stupid again. What difference did that make? Her stomach felt sick. Everything was changing too fast.

Lucious grinned. "I gotta work. I'll be back, though. Promise. We can talk then."

Act Nine

Scene One

After drying herself, Eve curled up on Lucious's tiny, unmade sofa bed. She hadn't realized she'd fallen asleep until she awoke to find him lying next to her. She jumped.

"Relax," Lucious said, pulling Eve toward him. "Nobody's going to bother you here." He lay on his side, his head resting against the pillow, his body facing Eve.

They stared at one another. Eve counted the passing seconds in heartbeats.

"I'm going to miss you, Eve." Lucious broke the silence, reaching for her, pulling her into a hug.

Outside, the sky went from purple to black. Rain fell in satiny sheets. Thunder rattled the windowpanes.

She felt so warm and safe in his arms. Then he kissed her softly, until her lips parted and the kiss grew more urgent.

"I don't know, Lucious. I don't think I should be here," Eve said, her words muffled against his neck as he held her to him. Her body was giving her a thousand signals, but, even though she'd brought the condoms, now she wasn't so sure. Still, she let him pull her closer, and closer. The thunder mixed with the thud of her heart, and the air in the tiny room sizzled. His voice was ragged. "I've liked you for a while. I wish things could have been different, you know? Now I'm leaving, and everything is changing and . . ."

He pulled her down on top of him and kissed her some more. They were operating at a level of pure need.

Soon they were rolling around, tugging at each other's clothes. Eve had the crazy thought that she'd never realized how much this was like wrestling. She was breathing real hard by the time she was down to her bra and panties.

Thud.

Not her heart this time. His belt buckle, still in his jeans when they hit the floor. He was everywhere all at once—beside her, across the room turning off the lights, lighting a candle.

"The storm's going to knock the power out, anyway. Always does." His voice sounded so unfamiliar, Eve found herself blinking hard in the darkness to make sure it was Lucious.

He returned to the bed. His body pushed against hers, and Eve felt something hot on her leg.

Oh, sweet Jesus, he's naked!

The image of Al standing on the back porch rubbing her back filled her. "No," she said, tugging at the sheet.

"I need you so much," Lucious said. He rolled onto his side, and expertly, without Eve's realizing how, managed to slide beneath her. She tried to keep from looking at him. She had only taken the birth-control pills Ma had tried to force down her throat a couple of times.

And here was Lucious, saying how much he wanted her, saying how much he needed her. Did that mean he loved her?

The kisses came in torrents, one after another after another after another, and Lucious continued to move his hands over her back, "Relax. I need you so much," he repeated.

He had undone her bra when Eve heard herself ask, "Lucious . . . do you love me?"

He never looked up. The nakedness he had hidden under the cover was coming to life, pushing to be free. And just as easily as he'd slipped beneath her, Lucious rolled on top.

Eve parted her lips to speak, but he smothered her mouth with kisses so hard she couldn't think. In the farthest reaches of her mind, she heard a muffled sound, then realized his hand was groping over the edge of the bed in search of something.

"Oh, man, I-I'll be right back. Damn!" Lucious thudded

to the bathroom. Panting, Eve realized he was looking for condoms.

"Lucious?" he didn't seem to hear. Not wanting him to come in and catch her bare butt walking around the room, Eve reached over the side of the bed. Her fingers caught the strap of her bookbag.

"We should be safe, you know?" he was mumbling, coming out of the bathroom.

"Looking for these?"

He stared, blinking in the shadowy candlelight.

"I bought them for you. For us." Eve held out the condoms.

"Oh, Baby," Lucious said. He climbed onto the sofa bed and opened the box.

"Lucious, do you love me?" She held the sheet up to her chin. Candlelight made his serpent tattoos appear to slither. He stared at her for a second.

"I'll always care for you, Eve; you know that."

She wanted more, but before she could speak, his warm hands slid beneath her bra, and she released a tight moan, sinking back against the wall. Lucious ripped at the condom. Paper rattled, and he took the little yellow rubber, golden in the glow of the candle, and inched it up where it belonged. Eve kept her eyes closed tight. One of them, anyway.

He pulled her, and she was beneath him again.

"Ow!" she cried out. The pain was sharp. She realized the pain had come from his falling onto her hair, which was spread out on the pillow.

"Sorry."

Lightning flashed, and, for a moment, electric light skittered across the trees in the world beyond Lucious's window.

"Lucious, wait," Eve cried, scrambling to her feet.

"What are you doing? Please, Eve, you can't leave me here like this," he said, flipping onto his side. Outside the window, a small halo of fire burned. Eve squinted. Was that a bush on fire?

Eve yanked her bra on and grabbed her bookbag. Lucious caught her wrist.

"Do you get off on this, Eve? Huh? Are you some kind of tease?" Lucious's whisper scratched against her earlobe like sandpaper.

"Do you love me, Lucious?"

"What? Why do you keep asking me that? Why does it have to be all about love?"

"You're naked, and you want to have sex with me. What is that about if it's not about love?"

"But I need you." He reached for her, and she pulled away, causing her bookbag to hit the radiator. A metallic ring filled the room, then a tiny thunk rattled against the floor. Eve's locket.

"I dropped my locket," she said, bending to her knees and sweeping her arm back and forth under the bed. Lucious groaned, rolled to one side, and turned the lamp switch.

"C'mon, Eve. Please, don't go," Lucious said.

Eve kept swatting the floor beneath the sofa bed. "I've got it," she said. The gold locket dangled between Eve's fingers, and she realized it had popped open.

"What . . . what is this?" she said, squinting at the tiny picture inside the locket. She didn't have a picture inside her locket. Eve got closer to the little lamp, still squinting. When she turned to Lucious, her eyes were dark and narrow.

"When did you do this? When?"

She got so close that she was in Lucious's face, holding the locket under his nose.

"What are you . . ."

"Look at it, Lucious. It's a miniature sketch."

"That's you. Right." He was sputtering, scampering upright.

Eve swung at him, but he ducked. "This is not me. It's Al. This has to be Al's locket. It's true; isn't it? You're her baby's father!"

Lucious stared in dazed silence. Finally he said, "Please, Eve, don't . . ."

But she was on her knees again frantically searching

beneath the bed. Within seconds she withdrew her hand, this time holding a second locket.

After inspecting the second one she said, "This one is mine."

She swung at Lucious again, this time connecting.

"Stop!" he yelled. He tried to sound tough and cool, but Eve decided she couldn't be intimidated by a naked boy with a shrinking condom dangling in front of him.

"You're the father of Al's baby!"

"I told you . . ."

"Told me what? What? WHAT?"

Lucious looked down at his shrinking condom as though he feared that once it shrank, he'd never grow it back up again. "It should never have happened."

When he said it, finally said it, he sounded exhausted.

"When I first stepped to her, I . . ."

"You thought she was me?"

He nodded. "You both worked at the park. I . . . you were cute, and I thought maybe we could . . ." His voice broke. Then he went on, "She was wearing that stupid hat. I thought she was you. I asked her to braid my hair. Soon as we started talking, though, I knew she thought I was . . . I wasn't good enough for her."

Eve stumbled around the bed, banged her toe, yanked on her clothes. A sick feeling in her stomach made her knees wobble. She remembered the day Al had borrowed one of her hats. Al had missed her appointment at the hairdresser and needed a relaxer touch-up.

"Don't go. Where're you going?"

"Home," Eve said. Big bursts of thunder rattled the windowpanes as she stepped into her shoes.

"I'm so sorry. So sorry. I didn't want it to be like this, you know?" Lucious said. "Please, let me explain."

Through the window, Eve saw that the fiery halo was not a burning bush. It was just a bunch of sticks and brush on the ground. Even if it wasn't a burning bush, Eve felt certain she'd been shown a sign. Well, Eve didn't need a sign. She knew what she had to do. "I'm going home," she said. She ran out the door and down the stairs, away from Lucious.

All the houses on her block were dark. The storm had knocked out all the power. Streetlights swung wildly in the driving rain. Eve was drenched. She couldn't possibly absorb any more water.

The kitchen door stood open inside the back porch. Eve stomped mud off her feet. Jelly Bean sat just inside the kitchen, a bandage on his furry leg. As Eve passed by, the dog lifted his head for a good scratch.

"Good boy," Eve said.

Voices, urgent and tense, came from the blackened living room. Eve inched through the swinging door and saw a thick knot of shadows huddled on the floor.

What now?

"Push," Ma yelled.

Al was lying flat on her back, and Ma was on her knees in front of her. Wetness penetrated Eve's clothes and dripped down her hair into her eyes. Cally, Aunt Mary's friend, was bent over Al. She and Ma turned to look up at Eve.

"The phones are out," Ma called over her shoulder.

"Omigod, Al, are you all right?" Eve rushed into the room and dropped to her knees. Al reached up and squeezed her hand.

"It hurts, Eve," she said. Her face was dark and sweaty. Her knees were bent, and her legs were open.

"Al, I can't get through to emergency on my cell right now, so it looks like we're on our own." Cally's voice was calm. When she leaned over, her billowy, auburn hair brushed Eve's face.

A sharp pain stabbed Eve right under her navel. She looked at Cally. How hard it must be for Cally to be here delivering Al's baby when her own baby had died.

Eve believed the stab of pain had been empathy; then she felt it again. Al wailed. She twisted Eve's fingers.

After all of the fighting and isolation, Eve knew that what she was feeling now were the goofy, twin powers that people talked about sometimes. The almost psychic connection that existed between twins. Eve felt her own fists knot in unison with Al's. When Al shuddered, so did Eve.

Ma had pushed up Al's nightgown over her belly. Eve noticed a dark puddle pooling on the sheet beneath her sister. Al squeezed Eve's hand so hard that Eve cried out. Cally instructed Eve to find candles. When Eve returned and lit them, Ma said the baby was crowning.

"The head, I see the head. Push," Ma repeated. Ma and Cally were shoulder to shoulder.

Eve tried not to look, but couldn't help herself. In the gray, dim, candle-lit room, on her mother's sheet, between her sister's bloody knees, a baby was making its way into the world. Eve crawled around to Al's side and continued to massage her shoulder and let her sister squeeze her hands.

"You're doing good, Al; you're doing good," Eve said, her voice coaching. She was unable to take her eyes off the tight, dark ball of squishy, squirmy life that was pushing its way into the world. In a few minutes the baby was all the way out. Cally scooped some goop out of its mouth and spanked her. Nothing.

"Oh, Jesus!" Ma said.

Cally swatted the baby again.

Thunder and wind slammed the far side of the house. The baby in Cally's arms remained silent.

Al's grip tightened on Eve. The air in the room grew thick and silvery with humidity and tension. Eve felt a fresh, hot rush of tears on her lids. The prayer that leaped to mind was not perfunctory or rehearsed. She begged and pleaded that God would spare the life of the small, infant girl.

Cally smacked the baby's bottom. The sound was hollow, distinct.

A rush of quiet, then a whisper of wind.

Howling. The baby wailed.

"She's crying," Ma said. The lights flickered, came on for a moment, then went back off. "Eve, run down the block and see if you can find somebody with a phone working. We still need to get Al and the baby to a hospital."

Scene Three

Scene Three

In her hospital bed, Al napped while Eve sat in the chair next to her. When she awoke, Eve told her all about Lucious and what had happened. "He's not a bad guy, he really isn't, but what we were going to do, I-I didn't feel right about it."

"I didn't, either," Al said with a sigh. "But I was so busy trying to prove a point, I lost sight of everything."

She looked tired. Eve stood. "Maybe I should go," she said.

Al reached for her hand. "Cally and Tom are going to adopt the baby." The lights flickered for a moment. Al turned on her side. "I'm glad, you know. I mean, at least she won't be with strangers. Maybe one day . . ."

Al drew in a deep breath. "Maybe one day they'll tell her who I am, so she won't have to wonder. Maybe one day she'll understand that what I did was best for her."

"I'm proud of you, Al," Eve whispered.

"Thanks. I'm proud of you, too. They did let me name her."

"Yeah? What name?"

"I named her Faith. Even though she won't be with me, Faith will always be part of my life now. When I think about giving up, when I want to question faith, I will always think of her. And when I do, I'll have to believe in powers greater than anything on Earth."

With that, Al began to sob. Eve sat down next to her and held her in her arms, held her until they both fell asleep.

Eve drove beside her mother. Al was napping off and on in the backseat. Daddy would be arriving later that night. Cally and Tom had taken the infant girl, Faith, home with them.

Ma said, "From the moment Al told me about her situation, all I kept thinking about was how I let my own mama down. How I followed my heart back in high school and had sex with a boy I thought would marry me. I didn't get pregnant, but your grandma Peaches made me feel so . . . ashamed."

Ruth Ann paused. The only sound she made for several moments was shallow breathing. She finally cleared her throat and spoke again, her voice softer. "I promised myself that if I was blessed with daughters of my own, I wouldn't ever try to make them feel the way Mama made me feel. Then she died, and I wound up trying to remake myself to prove that I deserved her love . . ." Her voice broke, and she bit off a sob.

Eve glanced at her mother in disbelief. "Ma, Grandma Peaches was a nut. Really, a nut. We weren't just her family, Ma. We were her victims."

To Eve's surprise, Ruth Ann's shoulders moved up and down, but she wasn't crying. She was laughing. With a shake of her head, she said, "I've spent the last three or so years killing myself to change the mind of a woman who is not only dead but had lost her mind long before she passed, God rest her soul."

"Amen to that," said Eve as her mother pulled to a stop sign.

Ma twisted her body to look over at Al in the backseat. "Everything is going to work out, though. It'll be fine. You'll see. You girls will both make me proud, and you'll be closer than ever."

Eve met her mother's gaze. This was Ma's way of apologizing. As close as she could come.

Ma pulled her shoulders straight, then said, "God will bless you with children one day, then you'll know how hard it is to make the right choices all the time."

Out of the corner of her eye, Eve saw the determined yet sincere set of her mother's jaw. She would remember that posture, that pose, for some future stage performance.

Scene Four

Scene Four

Proper farewells require large meals. Aunt Mary insisted upon a big, going-away dinner at the farm. Eve was headed to the New York acting workshop. And that wasn't all.

Ma had made a few phone calls. Eve was now on the waiting list for the fall term at the performing-arts high school across the lake. Eve wasn't quite sure what had changed between her and Ma—and Al. But since the birth of the baby, Ma had seemed calmer. Less angry and controlling.

She hadn't apologized, not outright. Instead Ma had asked Eve a ton of questions about the workshop. She'd called Glow Worm and Joel Cryer. One day while they were washing vegetables, Ma told Eve, "I think going to that workshop might be good for you. It helps a girl to mature when she can see what it's like to live on her own."

Just like that, Ma had managed to make it sound like a summer at a New York acting workshop had been her idea all along.

As for Al, Ma and Daddy had made a deal. Al would go to the University of Michigan for a year. When her year was over, she could come home and discuss whether or not she wanted to continue or whether she would, in Ma's words, "pursue the arts."

Aunt Mary's living room was full. It was the same cast that had come for Christmas, with a few special guest appearances. Tom and Cally Shepherd introduced Faith Shepherd, the six-pound baby girl with a new last name. Eve and Al held hands almost the entire time. Little Faith gurgled and wiggled. There would be an open adoption, one in which the two families could be involved with the child's life. Cally looked radiant; Al looked overwhelmed by the tearful show of gratitude.

Another special guest, timid at first, found a place near the small child. Lucious, back in Eden just for the weekend, had asked—no, begged—for the chance to see the child. His child. Lucious asked to hold her. He had met the Shepherds once, when their lawyer brought over the papers on which he signed away his parental rights.

Faith squirmed in Lucious's arms, and he made small, whispered promises. Eve and Al kept their fingers tangled together. Lucious set the baby down but remained mindful of Daddy's presence in the room. Daddy was watching him, a fact that kept the twins giggling most of the evening. Lucious inched his way over to the girls, then fished in his pocket for an envelope that he gave to Al. She studied it, opened it, and took out a check.

"What's this?" Al's nose wrinkled as she looked at the check for five hundred dollars drawn on Lucious's personal account.

"I worked two jobs so I'd be able to . . . well, I wanted to contribute something. I didn't know what else I could do since you didn't want me involved." He looked at the floor.

Al pushed the envelope back. "Lucious, I can't take your money. The Shepherds will take good care of Faith."

Lucious looked up and held Eve's eyes for a long moment. Daddy stepped over. Eve tried to move in and cut off his access to Lucious. Her father brushed past her.

"Take the money, Al," Daddy said. "Take it. A man's got a right to contribute to his child's life, no matter the circumstances."

Eve saw the look of relief wash over Lucious. Al called out, "Cally, we've got a late shower gift for you guys."

Later in the kitchen, the three teens who had shared so much drama over the past several months sat chatting at the kitchen table.

"Maybe one day we'll have a reunion on one of those talk shows where people with jacked-up histories get together and act ghetto," Lucious joked. They laughed easily. Eve ran her fingers through her newly cut hair.

"I still can't believe you cut your hair!" Al said. More giggling. The giggling felt good, like champagne bubbling up from their souls. Eve and Al dipped their heads until their identical haircuts brushed against one another. Lucious pulled something out of his pocket. A postcard.

"It's a reproduction of the centerpiece of my 'collection.' I couldn't have done it without you. Both of you," he said. The girls stared at the gray-and-sepia-toned card. A series of charcoal sketches of Eve and Al intertwined. Beneath the picture, raised black letters announced: *Differences. How to see contrasts when what the mind sees is identical.*

Both girls remained silent. Lucious was silent, too. Al's head rested on Eve's shoulder. Al said, "With your artsy genes and our flair for drama, it's scary to think of what Faith will be like when she's older."

Lucious nodded. "Yeah, scary."

When the dishes were put away and more good-byes exchanged, Bethany joined Eve in the upstairs bedroom. She'd come over to say her farewells, too. They folded the new sweaters Aunt Mary had given as gifts and hid secret tears because they'd made promises not to cry.

"He loves that baby so much, Lucious does. Seeing him with her, hearing him talk to Cally and Tom, I've never seen him that way," Eve whispered.

Bethany nodded. "I bet it hurts, right? Wanting him as much as you did for as long as you did, but knowing he was, you know, with your sister?"

Eve glanced around, making sure Al had gone. "You know what's funny? Today when he was here, it was the first time that I knew I definitely love him. I mean, I can truly say that I do. But not like what you might think. I'm glad we never . . ."

Eve was leaving within the hour for New York. Jelly Bean had gotten loose on the back porch and upset a wicker basket filled with rubber balls, baseballs, spongy balls, Super Balls, balls with swirly designs to mimic the earth's surface, along with balls in neon pink and yellow. All of the balls had scattered across the uneven grass in the backyard, which is why Eve was out in the yard hunting balls as though they were rare rubber caterpillars.

Eve spotted a few balls along the back hedge. She tossed one into the air. From where she stood, she could see the window to her bedroom, see the colonial shape of the house, and see the steps that Daddy had replaced to the back porch. Along the far wall were the plants she and Ma had planted several years ago. After years of neglect, several of the plants continued to sprout up and grow.

Cherry-red silk billowed and blossomed above the

back door. A silky flag. Al had made it when she was a freshman. She'd even won some sort of prize for it. *Funny,* Eve thought. She had never really looked at the house from this vantage point before, never even thought about it.

Through the kitchen window she could see Ma and Daddy packing boxes, probably food for their road trip. They were driving her to New York, a family road trip. Al was coming, too. She saw Al enter the kitchen and watched the shadowy pantomime of her family, unable to look away.

It seemed as if she'd spent her whole life sitting by that window looking out, trying to picture herself in the world beyond. Now here she was thinking about what it was like to be part of the world inside. A world where she shared her life with a family. She was part of something here. Here she knew who she was.

She was . . .

"Eve!" Daddy's voice boomed from the back door. "C'mon, Belly. It's time to go."

Eve waved and brushed herself off. The wind came up, and soft, satiny breezes ruffled her hair and whooshed past her ears. Summer's approach hung in the air, scented with wildflowers and fresh-cut grass. When she looked up, a fleeing cloud suddenly broke apart; one cloud became two identical clouds that drifted away until they hit a larger mass and became part of something bigger.

God was talking to her; Eve felt certain. This time she didn't ask or wonder about his meaning. She accepted her faith as a gift. Hadn't it been a lifetime ago that she'd prayed for a sign from God to lead her to Lucious? Hadn't it been a lifetime ago that she'd believed her only salvation from life in her small town would be either to get discovered as an actress or to escape by falling in love? Eve smiled at how easily her thoughts always became so dramatic.

Signs from God were supposed to tell her whether or not to have sex with a boy she loved from a distance. Her faith was supposed to heal the wounds in her and Al and Ma.

None of that seemed real now, not to the *real* Eve.

"Looks different already, doesn't it?" Al said, coming up alongside her. She was carrying Jelly Bean and scratching him behind the ears. Eve glanced at the kitchen window and realized Ma and Daddy had also stepped outside.

"I guess this is what I'll see in my head anytime I think of home," Eve said, her voice catching.

"With both of us going away, it'll be sort of nice, right? Coming home."

Eve reached over and scooped the doggie out of Al's arms before the sisters stepped onto the back porch. Daddy's voice boomed too loud, and Ma remained impeccable in her pressed and starched blouse and office attire despite preparing for the road trip.

They were as they had always been, yet they were changed, too, and would never be quite the same. Eve had her sister back, her mother, too. She had discovered a passion for acting and appreciated it as an art form rather than just as a means of escape. Eve had also learned that sometimes the biggest sign God can give you is the message he leaves in your heart. She had known all along that what she wanted with Lucious was a relationship, a deep, meaningful love connection— not just a one-night roll around his apartment. Eve was proud that in the end she'd made the decision not to have sex just to fulfill some romantic fantasy. She had made a choice.

Because of all of this, Eve had gained an even greater gift: She had been introduced to someone whom she looked forward to getting to know. The elusive, the incomparable, the one and only . . . Eve.

Another push of wind rustled the hair above her ears, and, just for a second, Eve could have sworn she heard the sweet, rapturous swell of applause.